Dream Desire

Realized

Ronald Bussey

Copyright

Copyright © 2025 by Ronald Bussey

All Rights Reserved.

No part of this book may be used or reproduced by any means, graphic, electronic, or mechanical, including photocopying, recording, taping, or by any information storage retrieval system without the written permission of the author, except in the case of brief quotations embodied in critical articles and reviews.

Because of the dynamic nature of the Internet, any web addresses or links contained in this book may have changed since publication and may no longer be valid.

The views expressed in this work are solely those of the author and do not necessarily reflect the views of the publisher, and the publisher hereby disclaims any responsibility for them.

Dedication

To my sons, Ronald Jr. and Michel,

who have carried my name and my legacy forward.

To my five grandchildren —

Alexie, Yannick, Cendryne, Maxyme, and Marc-

Antoine —

each of you a source of pride, inspiration, and unforgettable

joy.

To my great-grandchildren —

Nickky, Jackson, and Noa —

the promise of tomorrow, the continuation of our story.

You are the roots of my past and the wings of my dreams.
Through you, my journey continues — brighter, stronger,
everlasting.

Prologue

This book is not a biography. It is a reflection on what makes it possible to achieve our dreams and desires—even the most ambitious ones. The experience of an 80-year-old man shows that what may seem impossible to some can become attainable with determination.

According to Freud, dreams allow us to express and fulfil unfulfilled desires. In truth, dreams show us the future. Desire is the spark of the dream. The realization of that desire becomes the content of the dream. Desire is a powerful force that drives us to dream.

Achieving the impossible: a method to fulfil one's desires.

Since childhood, I've been driven by dreams that often seemed out of reach. But I never stopped believing in them. This book is the result of a journey, a quest for self-fulfillment shaped by the ups and downs of life.

Like many, my early years were guided by a thirst for discovery. Each day held the opportunity to learn, to grow, and to explore what seemed unreachable. And, like everyone, I had to face the limitations imposed by reality. But dreams are not mere escapes; they are guiding stars in the darkness.

What I've learned, I now wish to share. Because beyond my personal story, there are universal principles that can apply to anyone: believe in your aspirations, embrace challenges as lessons, and persevere even when the wind is against you.

There is no perfect path, no magic formula. But there is one thing we can all cultivate: the courage to take action for our dreams. And this book, I hope, will encourage you to believe in your own power of transformation.

Ronald Bussey

To contact the author:
dreamdesirerealized@gmail.com

PART ONE

Chapter 1: Learning to Build

I was born on June 17, 1945, in Verdun, in a modest red-brick house, as the city gathered for the Corpus Christi procession. The world was celebrating—and I was entering life. The youngest of three children, I grew up in a bilingual household—a Francophone mother and an Anglophone father—which taught me adaptability from the very start. From the age of five, I felt a natural curiosity for business. My mother, a cashier at the Savoy cinema, opened a small restaurant next door. Her entrepreneurial spirit left a mark on me. I watched her, and I learned. My first "business ventures" were modest: selling chalk, collecting milk bottles, and helping customers carry their bags. But the core idea was already there—offer the constraint that shapes service, find solutions, and earn a reward.

I discovered cinema thanks to my mother. Too young to go to school, the Savoy Theatre became my daycare. Sitting up in the balcony, I watched cowboy movies and Tarzan films. Those stories opened up unsuspected horizons for me. Later, I realized that passion drives us to surpass ourselves and that it is often the very first engine of great achievements. Collège Laval... The classical curriculum was not my place. But at home, my father's will reigned: he wanted me to become a lawyer or a doctor. Deep down, I dreamed of something else. The aptitude tests pointed me toward commerce, but that mattered little compared to his expectations. So, I clenched my teeth. I worked hard, often reluctantly, and finished my rhetoric with the greatest of struggles.

What I didn't know at the time was that those years, uncomfortable as they were, were giving me an invisible treasure: a determination that would never leave me. I was learning that one could suffer through effort, but also forge an inner armor.

Lesson 1: Perseverance and Passion

Small ideas are seeds of the future. Even failures—like being reported by the grocer—taught me to bounce back without giving up.

In high school, I ran for student vice president despite slim chances against an insider candidate. I lost, but I learned the value of taking risks and getting involved. It was my first contact with politics and public life.

During the summers, I worked on CN trains, rising from dining car server to maître d'hôtel. That job gave me financial freedom—but more importantly, it taught me discipline, service, and time management.

Lesson 2: Work Means Freedom

Work isn't just about earning a living. It builds character, develops skills, and opens horizons.

Another formative experience was playing Bonhomme Carnaval in Laval. It wasn't just a costume—I discovered the behind-the-scenes of event planning, logistics, and responsibility. At only 21, I was offered the chair of the committee.

Lesson 3: To Organize is to Influence

Behind every successful event is invisible planning and people working together for a shared goal.

Around that time, I began to meet influential people—politicians, entrepreneurs, and radio hosts. Their presence fascinated me. I tried my hand at radio, even turning down a job that was too far from home. Still, the experience helped me hone my speaking, persuasion, and personal branding skills.

In 1969, I took part in my first political campaign as a youth organizer for a mayoral candidate. It was an incredible learning experience: I discovered the importance of teamwork, grassroots work, and building community ties.

Lesson 4: Nothing Happens Alone

In politics, as in business, success rests on solid teams mobilized around a clear purpose.

When CN offered me a permanent position, I said no. It was not out of recklessness, but because it didn't feel right. Instead, I ventured into an unknown field—consumer lending. Quickly promoted, I bought my first house at 22. But after four years, I felt trapped. I left everything. No job, no unemployment benefits. Six months of uncertainty.

Lesson 5: Dare to Take Risks

I learned that you can bounce back if you believe in yourself and accept the discomfort of temporary uncertainty.

Eventually, I was hired as a pharmaceutical sales representative. I had no formal training, but I had charm,

English, and a customer-focused mindset. That job allowed me to grow, to travel, and to master the art of selling and listening. Within a few years, I became the top salesperson in the country.

Every step, every choice, and every setback helped shape the man I became. Learning doesn't only happen in school—it happens through observation, trying, failing, and getting back up. It means believing that no matter where you start, you can always go further.

That was when I understood something essential: security does not guarantee happiness. What drives us is our inner momentum, our movement, and our belief in ourselves. Risk can be frightening—but stagnation scared me more.

It's easy to follow well-worn paths, to settle into a comforting routine. But only by daring to change direction and face uncertainty can we discover what we're truly capable of. Fear is a travel companion, not an enemy. And each risk I took brought me closer to my dreams.

Entrepreneurship, politics, travel—everything I achieved later took root in those early decisions. That period of my life was a time of intense learning—not from books, but from action, challenges, and real life.

I had learned six major lessons:

- **Perseverance** to not give up after failure.
- **Passion** to push oneself beyond limits out of love for what one does.
- **Work** to build with effort and discipline.
- **Organization** to gather, structure, and move ideas forward.
- **Teamwork** to understand that no one succeeds alone.
- **Risk** to move forward despite fear.

These lessons would become the pillars of everything I would undertake. They gave me the tools to act and the courage to envision a future worthy of my desires.

Because a dream is not realized through thought alone but through action, and that action was about to propel me toward my greatest youthful ambition: politics.

All these early learnings made me a curious, motivated, and ambitious young man. I didn't have a clear plan for the future yet, but I knew I wanted something different. I wasn't destined for an ordinary life. Something inside me was burning—a strong desire to surpass myself.

I read a lot. I was inspired by great historical figures, builders, and leaders. Then one day, I discovered the books of Dr. Joseph Murphy—and it changed everything. His *"The Power of Your Subconscious Mind"* opened my eyes to the power of thought and gratitude. One more essential lesson was added to my foundation:

Lesson 6: Gratitude

Say thank you, even in hard times. Be thankful for the little things. Gratitude attracts positivity.

Chapter 2: Dare to Get Involved

At the age of 26, I had already learned seven life lessons. Now it was time to put them into practice and see where they would lead me. My greatest dream: to enter politics. To refuse passivity. To choose not to be a mere spectator, but to become an actor of change. To nurture the desire to influence the people around us, to defend ideas, to make a difference, and to give a voice to those who have none.

Politics is a platform to defend those who don't have a microphone. It is not reserved for an elite: it belongs to all who want tomorrow to be better than today. It begins with indignation, with an idea, with a dream. And if it is sincere, it can change the world. In short, politics is about helping people.

The Saint-François district included three parishes: Saint-François-de-Sales, Notre-Dame-du-Sourire, and Saint-Noël-Chabanel. In the fall of 1972, Dr. Lucien Paiement, vice-chairman of the executive committee, was preparing to challenge Mayor Jacques Tétreault, who was finishing his second term. Paiement launched a public consultation to measure the satisfaction of Laval citizens with the current administration.

He summoned me, along with seven or eight other residents of Saint-François. Wanting to form a team to support his bid against the incumbent mayor, he sought to gauge Laval's opinion of his candidacy. He showed us a plastic briefcase bearing the words 'Opération Action' in bold letters. Inside was a questionnaire we were to use during door-to-door visits. Saint-François was divided into five sectors, and one was entrusted to me.

When someone asked Paiement who his candidate would be for Saint-François if he decided to run, he replied vaguely, promising nothing. He concluded the meeting by announcing that the results would be revealed at a large rally in the spring.

At the famous April rally, fifty of my supporters from Saint-François joined me. Paiement unveiled the results of Operation Action: 60% of Laval residents wanted a change in the current administration. Unsurprisingly, he announced his candidacy and presented the public with all the candidates elected in 1969 with Jean-Noël Lavoie's team. He was counting on support from the west of the city, but needed to win the east to become mayor.

Since he had sent me no signal, I waited a week before meeting with him. I still hoped to be chosen, but instead, he introduced me to his candidate for Saint-François—a resident of Notre-Dame-du-Sourire and a Parti Québécois organizer—and asked me to support him. Offended, the salesman in me came out. I made an impromptu plea for my candidacy, pointing out that I had already gained enough ground to be elected as an independent and that my team was ready for the campaign.

I reminded him that my stronghold was precisely in Notre-Dame-du-Sourire, where I had grown up. Shaken, Paiement asked for a month to reflect.

In early June, he met with me again. I explained that I had already secured two out of three parishes; only Saint-Noël-Chabanel remained, the most populated one, home to the sitting councilor and the head of the local credit union. My arguments were convincing—he accepted my candidacy.

I had no idea what the work of a councilor truly involved. I had never attended a municipal meeting. But why get into politics? Because I believed a politician had the power to change things. I also felt our neighborhood was being neglected compared to others. A founder by nature, stubborn, a good salesman, and very sociable, I believed politics was for me. As a citizen, you depend on your city;

that's where decisions about services, sports, and parks are made—and I wanted to be part of those decisions.

Now all that was left was to win under his banner.

'With Paiement, Things Will Change.'

Photo Election 1973

To win Saint-François, I had to fight against a reserved man, confident of his victory. Without shame, he kept repeating that I was nothing but a 'young, inexperienced kid.'

In July, I decided to meet, one by one, two or three influential people from each of the three parishes. Whether for or against me, I wanted their honest opinion on my chances. Without exception, they all told me I had none. But I wasn't discouraged. I made them a promise: at the end of August, September, and October, I would return to ask again. Each time, I evaluated my progress. And the more my chances improved, the more these influential people—a garage owner, a convenience store owner, my barber, a school commissioner—talked about me.

By early August, Paiement gathered the candidates at his headquarters on Saint-Martin Boulevard. It was there that I first met elected officials and other candidates. I knew no one. I soon realized there were several candidates in Laval's 14 districts; only Saint-François and Laval-sur-le-Lac had a single candidate. I understood that if I, the risk-taker, failed, Paiement might lose a district.

At one meeting, Paiement announced that each candidate had to contribute $1,000 to the campaign fund and raise $5,000 from local businesspeople. The $1,000 didn't bother me—I wrote the check on the spot—but I refused to raise money. He explained I could approach contractors with city contracts—garbage collection, snow removal. I refused, not wanting to owe anyone favors. I told him my father knew his chief fundraiser personally, which surprised him. I had not anticipated this financial aspect, even if I suspected the party collected funds across Laval.

I launched my campaign in early August. Organized and disciplined, I followed a strict schedule: weekdays, 8 a.m. to 4 p.m., I worked for Wyeth. From 4 p.m. to 6 p.m., I knocked on doors in the district. From 7 p.m. to 9 p.m., I held kitchen meetings—in the homes of my supporters, where neighbors were invited to hear my vision. Afterward, I returned to my chief organizer's office for strategy sessions with my team.

On weekends, we canvassed in groups of five or six volunteers. I also made a point to visit anyone who wanted to speak to me. We needed volunteers for each section, phone callers for canvassing, drivers to bring voters to the polls, and supervisors for voting stations. My personal goal: to knock on every door. At each visit, I handed out a business card with 'With Paiement, Things Will Change,' along with photos and my phone number. If no one answered, I left a handwritten note.

Three months and one pair of worn-out shoes later, I could say: Mission accomplished.

By late August, my contacts told me I was beginning to be known. By late September, I was nearly tied with my opponent. By late October, they believed I had strong chances of winning. Toward the end, at candidate meetings, Paiement held me up as an example of hard work. Ten days before the election, he confirmed what I had told him all along: a poll predicted my victory.

On November 4, at 7 p.m., the polls closed. While officials and my representatives counted the votes, I went to my organizer's place with about ten others. Even though victory seemed likely, doubt remained. The wait felt endless. I sweated, tense to the maximum, but tried to appear calm. At 8 p.m., when the first results came in, I saw I was leading in every section.

The stress vanished, replaced by indescribable euphoria. The phone rang: my opponent conceded and congratulated me. I didn't yet realize the magnitude of what had happened.

You can work for years to become a councilor, live fully in your neighborhood, be a founding member of the Optimist Club of Saint-François, a Knight of Columbus, president of the Laval Carnival, director of the Homeowners' League, or even write monthly articles for the local paper.

I was truly invested in my city and my district. Before the election, I had resigned from my positions as Carnival president and League director to focus fully on this new chapter.

At some point, you must choose: remain in the comfort of the known, or dare to move toward something greater, more demanding—but also more meaningful.

To be involved is not just to hold titles. It is to give of yourself. To wake up each morning with the desire to improve what surrounds you, to serve a cause bigger than yourself.

Sometimes this involvement becomes a calling. A force pushing you to take a new step. That's how I felt: that everything I had done until then had prepared me for this moment—the moment you decide not just to participate, but to take responsibility and act fully, in plain sight.

You dream, you visualize, you rally hundreds of people to your cause, you convince them you will win, you take huge risks—and when you succeed, the adrenaline peaks. You feel joy and pride, yet you can hardly believe it.

That night, we headed to Laval Catholic High School in Chomedey, where Paiement's team gathered. Escorted by two officers, we entered the school. On stage, Paiement presented his councilors. The youngest councilor in Laval had just been elected with more than 66% of the vote: Ronald Bussey, from Saint-François.

I climbed onto the stage to applause, shook hands with the new mayor, and congratulated him. Paiement's team took power with 23 out of 24 councilors, including only one woman. Laval's third mayor stepped onto the scene. After years of work and volunteering, I had achieved my dream.

Later, I realized that running for election requires both courage and humility. You win or you lose.

Being elected is the beginning of another marathon. The real race starts after victory. Citizens expect you to deliver. Every call, every complaint, and every question deserves an answer. As a counselor, I had to live up to the trust placed in me.

And it was then that I learned a new life lesson, one I had not anticipated:

Lesson 8: To Serve

Not to serve yourself, but to serve others. To listen, even when tired. To carry hopes, manage frustrations, seek solutions. Politics, at its core, is not a title—it is a commitment.

I remember one cold autumn evening, going door to door. An elderly woman opened cautiously. I spoke gently, without trying to convince her. At the end, she said: 'I haven't voted in 20 years. But for you, I will. Because you took the time.' Moments like that mark you for life.

I was not perfect. I made mistakes and learned along the way. But I never betrayed my values. And looking back, I know I was right to dare.

To those who hesitate to get involved, I say this: don't wait to be experts. Don't wait to be invited. The impulse comes from within. Society doesn't need spectators—it needs builders.

And if this chapter inspires in you even a small desire to act, then it has served its purpose.

Chapter 3: Power

I was 28, had a job at Wyeth that I loved, and had just been elected as a municipal councilor for Laval. The swearing-in took place a week later, followed by the appointment of the executive committee members. Shortly after, we had our first caucus, aimed at explaining how the city worked, our role as councilors, and introducing us to the municipal officials.

From this first contact with the system, they made us understand an implicit reality of power: at Christmas, we would receive gifts—liquor, gift baskets, or other presents. He clearly told us that we did not have to refuse them or call the donors to thank them. It was customary, a kind of tacit acknowledgment of our status as elected officials in Laval. A barely veiled message about how the gears of power and the relationships between politics and influence worked.

Over the months, the mayor's chief of staff regularly offered me free tickets to shows or social events. I was new to this world, and to me, this was power: privileges, facilitated access, and instant social recognition that came with the status. But I would quickly come to understand that true power did not lie in those favors but in the ability to decide and influence.

From the very start of my term, I took my role as a councilor very seriously. I was interested in the major files under review, in the future and development of Laval, and particularly in my district, Saint-François. Yet I quickly discovered another aspect of power: it was not equally distributed among elected officials. The real decisions were made in the executive, often behind closed doors, between the mayor and the executive, and one of the members was Gilles Vaillancourt.

Each month, before the city council meeting, we had a caucus. In 1974, during one of these meetings, the mayor arrived with a proposed zoning change to allow a new quarry on Saint-Elzéar Road. As usual, no one spoke. Silence was the norm. But this time, I spoke up:

— Why open a new quarry? We already have dust and noise problems with the ones we have.

The mayor didn't seem to appreciate my comment. He replied sharply:

— Elections are expensive, and some people helped us.

It was a moment of revelation. Behind public decisions hid a network of private interests. My comment struck a chord: the councilor of the affected district also started asking questions. For the first time, the mayor faced open disagreement. Yet, during the official meeting, the vote was unanimous in favor of the quarry. The machinery of power had prevailed, sweeping aside individual objections.

During that first four-year term, I learned the hard way what exercising power in municipal politics meant. Often in disagreement with certain regulations or the development vision for Laval, I frequently spoke during caucuses. This earned me a reputation as a troublemaker. Many of my colleagues saw me as someone whose questions could be unsettling.

In this political world, silence was more valued than opinion. Yet I couldn't bring myself to become a passive elected official. When decisions didn't serve citizens, I couldn't stay silent. I was disruptive, but I was representative. And that was my duty.

Surviving in an environment where the rules of the game don't match our core values is a challenge that directly tests our integrity and emotional endurance. One can feel isolated, disillusioned, and powerless—sometimes even betrayed.

You need to have a clear and personal vision of why you're there—what you want to defend and who you're fighting for. In my mind, I was chosen by my citizens, so it was for them that I fought. I was surrounded by friends, a loyal team, and honest people. I often took a step back from my colleagues to avoid being contaminated. You have to accept that not everything can change immediately and learn how to maneuver your convictions.

One day, the mayor said to me with a smirk:

— I see you're not happy. Prepare a document on your vision of the role of a councilor.

I seized the opportunity:

— Ok! Give me a month, and I'll come back with recommendations.

My determination forced him to act. He created a committee of four councilors, including myself. A month later, we submitted a series of suggestions, all of which were implemented: the creation of an office with secretarial support for councilors at City Hall, publication of the executive committee meeting dates, and sending the agenda 24 hours before those meetings.

This was my first concrete victory. I had just discovered that even within a rigid system, you could create a breach. Power, when used wisely, can become a lever for transformation.

As the 1977 elections approached, my employer, Wyeth, appreciating my sales skills, offered me the territory of my dreams: Laval, northern Montreal, and the Terrebonne region up to Rawdon. I couldn't have asked for better—combining my professional career with my passion for politics.

I was convinced I'd be re-elected. I had worked relentlessly since 1973. But another ambition was growing in me: to join the executive, where real decisions were made. I had discussed it several times with the mayor, who remained evasive.

There too, I refused to remain silent. Knowing my files inside and out, I was the only councilor attending executive committee meetings, even though I wasn't a member. It was my way of showing that I wasn't just a figurehead. I was learning, observing, and preparing myself. Because one thing was clear: power is not given, it is taken.

Chapter 4: Know How to Seize Your Chance

In the spring of 1976, I experienced another major life lesson: knowing how to see an opportunity and, above all, how to seize it. It happened during a Wyeth convention held at the Auberge des Gouverneurs in Montreal. At the end of a day of training, I found myself at the bar with a few colleagues. We started chatting with some medical secretaries from Montreal. By pure chance, I began a conversation with one of them.

I told her that I lived in Laval and was a municipal councilor in Saint-François. She looked very surprised, then confided a professional secret. She explained that her boss was negotiating the purchase of a retirement home located on Montée Masson, in Saint-François. As it happened, I knew the owner well, as well as the residence in question. Pretending not to be surprised, I told her I knew the place and that it must be a significant transaction. Without hesitation, she shared the details.

Since my presidency of the Laval Carnival, I had dreamed of getting into business. Lying in bed, I reflected on this project. Why not make the purchase myself? A municipal councilor investing in his own community while being a medical representative—this would be a good deal. In a flash, I was convinced that if I acted quickly, I could beat the doctor to it.

My instinct told me that, as a medical rep, I often visited retirement homes and spoke with their owners. I saw successful people. One of my uncles even owned a similar establishment in Montreal. He was also doing very well.

The day after the convention, I decided to act. Even before speaking to my uncle, I wanted to meet the owner and express my interest. I went to the site without an appointment. At 4:30 p.m., I walked into the front office. A few minutes later, we were chatting in his basement apartment. He seemed surprised that the news had leaked, as he had hoped to keep the deal secret. He suggested coming to my house to discuss it further.

He expressed his disappointment with the buyer, who seemed intent on negotiating a lower price. I, on the other hand, stated that the amount seemed fair, but I would need time to gather the funds. He surprised me: he hoped I would become the next owner. He even handed me the financial statements from the past two years. That gesture was a turning point.

I discovered the salaries of nurses, attendants, kitchen and maintenance staff, and the food costs. It wasn't a private residence but a government-funded one, with 53 beds supported by a daily per diem from the State. A portion of the residents' pensions was also deducted. If expenses were well-managed, the surplus would go to the owners.

It's crazy to invest $200,000 without knowing if it's a good investment and where to find the money. Yet, my instinct told me I had to go for it. Taking risks is something you learn, but smart risks. When I ran for office, I learned there are always two outcomes: win or lose. A calculated risk means knowing the terrain, evaluating the chances, and believing the dream is achievable.

I knew nothing about care centers and didn't want to work there. But a phrase kept coming to mind:

Ronald, when nothing works, the answer is often right next to you. Never give up!

And part of the solution was indeed close by.

During a municipal council meeting, Yves, a notary and colleague, said to me:

— You seem deep in thought.

I told him about my project. He replied,

— I've always wanted to own a place like that. Come to my office tomorrow.

That was the breakthrough. Jacques, also present, asked:

— Can we buy it as a trio?

I answered,

— Better to have a third than nothing at all.

The deal was made, provided we respected the original price. We placed a $15,000 deposit, conditional on obtaining the transfer permit.

But that permit depended on the Ministry of Social Affairs... in the middle of the 1976 general election. What could we do? We proposed to the seller that he keep the deposit if there was no response before February 15, 1977. He agreed.

I then joined the campaign team of the PQ candidate in my riding. Officially, a municipal official was supposed to remain neutral, but I followed Lucien Paiement's example, who had been involved in previous elections. I accompanied my candidate around the neighborhood, visited the residence, and explained my project.

The mayor learned about my involvement. He summoned me to scold me for supporting a Péquiste and threatened me for the next election. Bad move. On November 15, 1976, René Lévesque won a historic victory. My candidate became a minister. I explained our situation to him. He submitted our file to his colleague, the minister of health, and the permit was signed during one of the first cabinet meetings.

Yes, there was some luck. But above all, there was conviction, perseverance, and a good dose of courage.

We created the company BBG: Yves became president, I was vice-president, and Jacques was the general manager. He ran the residence full-time. We kept it for sixteen years. Once the mortgage was paid off, we sold it in 1993 at a high price. Jacques retired. For us, it was the end of a chapter. But also, proof that sometimes, an opportunity—however small at first—can change an entire life.

Chapter 5: David Versus Goliath

Why take such a step? Why dare to stand against an incumbent mayor, a well-oiled machine, and a system that seemed unshakable? Because deep down, I could no longer be content with managing just one district. My commitment extended beyond Saint-François. I dreamed of a fairer city, closer to its citizens, where decisions wouldn't be made behind closed doors. I wanted to be among those who challenge the status quo, not those who settle into it.

Was I prepared for the 1977 elections? An opposition was already working to unseat the mayor and his councilors. A mayoral candidate emerged during the thaw, assembling his team. My opponent in Saint-François was one of the founders of the neighborhood's Optimist Club. I hardly campaigned. However, I was passionate about the struggle unfolding across the island and spent considerable time at our headquarters on St-Martin Boulevard, where I uncovered the secrets...

We won all 24 districts of the city, making us the first to achieve an uncontested victory at city hall. I was re-elected with a significant majority, but I didn't feel the same emotions as during my first election. For four years, I had worked so hard in my district that victory was almost assured.

The mayor reformed his committee as it was. I protested by boycotting the reception following our swearing-in. As a city councilor, I had seen it all. I wanted to know the real power, where decisions are made. Waiting four years to depend on the mayor was no longer acceptable. Managing my district was one thing, but contemplating a greater challenge was another. That's what I did for two years.

One day, I saw Lucien in the city hall lobby with a few councilors. He said to me, "You take good care of your district." I was on shaky ground. I replied that I saw myself on the executive committee, where I would be very effective. He said, "You're young; you have your whole future ahead of you." I tried to make him understand what I wanted, but I ended up telling him, "You didn't want me, so you leave me no choice but to oppose you in the next election." He and the other councilors laughed.

My decision was made. I had two choices: realize my dream and join the executive committee, or leave politics. My words were considered, but I felt the desire for new challenges. I had decided to try to realize my dream, even if failure was a possibility. One thing is certain: those who try nothing risk nothing. Self-confidence is essential to make the impossible possible. You have to believe in yourself to take action despite doubts.

All my life, I would struggle to hear a "no" or the word "impossible." In my mind, everything is possible. But our relationship deteriorated. At meetings, I asked questions that caught journalists' attention, with headlines like:

Bussey opposes the council.

My obstruction made me unpopular with other councilors.

I then felt that an opposition was forming among Lavallois, particularly because of the downtown project in Carré Laval. It was the perfect time to break this unanimity, which further motivated me to bring this opposition to life. Creating an opposition myself scared me. I thought it was too big a challenge, but the idea always fascinated me. After all, why not try? My entourage encouraged caution, but I knew it was too late to back down.

I decided to form a discussion group to assess Laval citizens' expectations and their vision for the city's future. This informal survey revealed that many were waiting for an opposition party. I had no intention of running for mayor, but if my team managed to unseat the mayor, I would have access to the executive committee, where power lies. Tackling the impossible always excited me. But why? After six years as an alderman, I found that Saint-François was neglected. A councilor, Achille Corbo, who also wanted to be on the executive, joined me.

A bill concerning elected officials' salaries was introduced. Mayor Lucien Paiement went to the commission chaired by Jacques Parizeau. Achille and I attended the hearings, particularly interested in the increase in elected officials' allowances and changes to the pension plan. Salaries were doubled, and allowances increased retroactively. The pension plan was modified. We were incredulous at these increases.

In November 1979, two years before the elections, the executive committee examined the municipal budget. I decided to oppose the proposed property tax increase. I advocated for spending cuts, notably canceling the neighborhood festival and the downtown project. The mayor refused to listen to reason, and I informed the press of my intention to vote against the budget adoption. The news made headlines, and I forced Lucien to make a decision.

Tension escalated. The mayor expelled us from his team, and we were now in opposition. It was hell, but we were ready to face it. The situation worsened when my proposal for budget cuts was rejected by 22 votes to 2. But the birth of a political opposition in Laval had just been confirmed.

This battle, which I compared to David versus Goliath, would last two years. After our defeat in the vote, Achille and I launched a petition to contest the municipal tax increase. We collected 50,000 signatures, almost as many as the number of votes in the last election. It was a masterstroke that marked a turning point.

On May 5, 1980, we presented our petition at City Hall. The room was filled with the mayor's supporters, but there were only two of us: Achille and me. The reaction was astounding. 50,000 signatures! It proved how dissatisfied Lavallois were with the current administration. The media and the public talked about it for weeks. Lucien Paiement still didn't understand the magnitude of our success.

The time had come to bring the opposition to life by creating a real political party. After several weeks of discussions, the name "PRO des Lavallois" for Parti de Ralliement Officiel was born. Our campaign wasn't easy, as we were alone against a well-oiled machine. But little by little, we advanced. Our first poll revealed that nearly 60% of Lavallois were dissatisfied with the mayor. The press announced that Lucien Paiement was in danger, and although the mayor doubted the quality of the poll, thus began our fight for change.

Chapter 6: Winning with the People

On Tuesday and Thursday mornings, I attended executive committee meetings. This annoyed the mayor, but these meetings were public. I studied the files and found material to raise questions during council meetings. I saw contracts being awarded to contractors, but one thing struck me: why does this entrepreneur never get any city contracts? His company, prosperous and well-established, worked for the provincial government.

One day, I decided to meet him. He was elegant, well-dressed, and had the temperament of a calm and thoughtful businessman. He hated the mayor and was delighted that I had reached out. He quickly offered to finance our campaign on the condition that his friend, Claude-Ulysse Lefebvre, be our candidate for mayor.

Claude-Ulysse, a former alderman from Duvernay, was a slender man with white hair that made him look older than his 52 years. His demeanor and artistic temperament gave him a certain charisma, but he was fairly broke. At our first meeting, tension rose between him and Achille. They both lived in Duvernay. Achille had known him since his time at city hall. Old disputes resurfaced. He saw us as fighters, and we knew he didn't realize that neither Achille nor I wanted to run for mayor. Jean-Louis claimed he could raise the necessary campaign funds.

The dilemma: I wanted to defeat Mayor Paiement. His power relied on a locked system—contractors close to power, a well-oiled network. But to beat him, we had to campaign seriously, with resources. And those resources often came from the same circles I was criticizing.

The entrepreneur and Claude-Ulysse Lefebvre were part of that system, too. They also had links to business, funding, and influence networks. Yet with them, I had a real chance to make a difference. The choice was clear but hard: stay in opposition and keep my principles intact... or accept a compromise for a shot at victory. I chose strategy—not out of naivety, but out of conviction that sometimes, to break a system, you must first enter it.

Building a Winning Strategy: I loved politics and working with Saint-François citizens to find solutions to their problems. From the beginning, I knew the system was controlled by fundraisers who, after the election, oversaw a circle of businessmen, engineers, contractors, lawyers, and notaries. It wasn't ideal, but it was the only way to win. After a year in opposition, Achille and I were convinced Paiement could be beaten, but we needed the right strategy.

Achille and I decided to share power with the newcomers. At our second meeting, the decision was made official. We formed a team: me as the organizer, Achille as my deputy on the council, a fundraiser, and a mayoral candidate. We quickly realized Claude-Ulysse was in a poor financial position and would need a salary to cover his expenses. For him, there was nothing to lose: if he won, he'd have a good salary and access to the circle of influence.

Claude had no intention of working hard; he relied on me to manage the city. Everyone assumed I would run for mayor. After our agreement, I spent a lot of time with Claude-Ulysse, who was a Liberal while I was a Péquiste. We contacted several communications firms, facing repeated rejections. Finally, the Parti Québécois recommended an agency we hired.

The communication experts assessed Claude-Ulysse: his appearance, charisma, and ease with public speaking made him a good candidate. They developed a communication and advertising plan for the months leading up to the election.

My role was to recruit a leader for each district, each responsible for assembling 25 people. Once done, we had a base of nearly 600 volunteers—the core of an effective electoral machine.

Momentum built. Our launch night at Buffet Lazio brought together 1,200 people and numerous journalists. Claude-Ulysse's speech focused on cutting spending and valuing neighborhoods, in contrast to the mayor's grand projects like Carré Laval.

We set up our headquarters on Saint-Martin Boulevard. I found an assistant whose partner became our secretary. My goal was to reach out to businesspeople and organizations opposed to the mayor. I negotiated a four-page ad space in a local paper to defend our ideas weekly.

We recruited motivated candidates who were less sensitive to criticism. I trained them on the importance of door-to-door canvassing, tailored to each district. In August, a poll alarmed us: Paiement had 32%, Claude-Ulysse 11%, and Bernard Roy, a third candidate for mayor, 3%, with over 50% undecided. By late September, we were still missing a candidate in Fabreville. We found a volunteer for $1,000. To everyone's surprise, he was elected on election night.

The Final Sprint: In September, we launched a major ad campaign with 24 billboards and radio spots. In October, we aired six TV ads, including one during a Canadiens–Nordiques game, featuring Claude-Ulysse as a caring father. Team Paiement, confident in their victory, ran no TV ads.

The final poll showed a close race: Paiement 22%, Claude-Ulysse 18%, Roy 9%, with still 50% undecided. Team Paiement challenged me to a $25,000 bet on their victory. Outraged by their arrogance, I doubled it to $50,000, but they preferred to keep it at $25,000 with a notary.

Two days before the election, we printed 100,000 copies of a flyer claiming that a vote for C.R.A.N. was a vote for Paiement. I like to think this swayed some undecided voters.

On November 1, 1981, convinced of victory, Paiement passed me and said, "We may lose one or two seats, but no more." I replied, "This is your last day as mayor."

The early results favored Paiement. But by 7 p.m., I was elected with 85% of the vote in my district. By 9 p.m., Claude-Ulysse had won the mayoralty with a 3,000-vote lead. We had elected 13 councilors to Paiement's 11.

The atmosphere at our HQ was electric. I was overwhelmed with emotion. For two years, while working full-time at Wyeth, I had organized this campaign, supported our candidates, and faced scorn from journalists and businesspeople. But the citizens of Laval believed in us.

This victory wasn't just a political shift. It was a revolution in municipal culture. It wasn't one man's win—it was the result of a network of engaged citizens. Every volunteer, every home visited, every hand shaken helped build that result. It wasn't me against Lucien—it was us against a closed system.

At 36, I had just achieved one of the greatest challenges of my life. I was about to be sworn in as vice-president of Laval's executive committee. This victory taught me that everything is possible and every problem has a solution. You just have to find it.

They say in politics, you must compromise to win. Maybe. But I believe you must rally, unite, mobilize. I won, yes—but with the people, not despite them.

You must do things you've never done to get results you've never had.

To celebrate this achievement, I left in February 1982 with two friends for a ten-day journey exploring Japan, Thailand, and Hong Kong.

We started with three days in Tokyo. Among the sites we visited, Shinjuku Gyoen offered a real oasis of greenery in the bustling Shinjuku district, known for its towering skyscrapers. This traditional Japanese garden stood in stark contrast to the surrounding dense urbanization. Walking beneath its majestic trees, my thoughts drifted to Carré Laval, the former quarry Lucien wanted to turn into a downtown core. Why not make it a vast green park for Lavallois instead?

Our trip continued in Thailand, where we explored Bangkok by tuk-tuk, the iconic and colorful mode of transport. This immersive experience gave us a feel for the city's vibrant energy—one of the most polluted cities in the world, with swarms of scooters weaving through the streets. After this urban plunge, we took a taxi to Pattaya, one of the country's biggest beach resorts, about 150 kilometers south of Bangkok, on the shores of the Gulf of Thailand. Its beaches and lively vibe make it a must-visit.

To wrap up our journey, we stopped in Hong Kong. Landing there is an experience in itself: as the plane descends, it feels like it's about to land right in the ocean, so close to the city's buildings. Once there, we rode the famous double-decker tram across the island and then took the funicular up to Victoria Peak. From the top, the panoramic view of the city and harbor is absolutely breathtaking. It was in Hong Kong that we did our shopping.

46

Chapter 7: The Wear of Power

It was three o'clock in the morning. Sleep had abandoned me, carrying away with it any peace of mind. I tossed and turned in bed, my eyes fixed on the ceiling, as if that empty space could provide an answer.

At 36 years old, I had just lived through one of the greatest adventures of my professional life, but already, an implacable choice awaited me at dawn.

The next day, I would have to give up a dazzling salary, the fruit of eleven years of loyalty and passion for Wyeth.

More than just a job, it was a part of my identity: a career I had built with relentless effort, successes I had savored, enviable perks — a company car, an expense account, the recognition of a great corporation.

All of that had its price, but also its flavor.

And yet, that same day, November 2, 1981, at Claude's request, I would take my place as Vice President of the Executive Committee of the City of Laval, managing the city full-time.

A position of responsibility, influence, and challenges —
but paid half of what I earned the day before.

There, too, another passion called me: the passion to
build, to transform, to serve a community rather than pursue
only material comfort.

Two passions, two worlds, two destinies. One acquired,
reassuring, almost natural. The other, uncertain, risky, but
burning with a new fire. My heart was torn: remain in the
safety of already-conquered success, or leap into the
dizzying unknown of a future yet to be invented.

A phone call that morning ended my doubts. Paul
Montreuil, on the other end, offered me more time — a
chance to breathe, to reflect again. But I knew that if I let the
moment pass, I would betray my own truth.

"— My decision is made, Paul."

The words came out with a strange force, a mix of relief
and pain.

For choosing is both winning and losing. That day, I paid
the price of power: giving up one passion to embrace
another, accepting that life sometimes demands we sacrifice
the comfort of what we love in order to leap toward what we
must become

As vice president of the executive committee, I worked with city officials to manage the city. Two secretaries at my disposal, a salary of $55,000, a new level of authority… but the reality remained: by leaving Wyeth, I had given up a higher salary and a company car — a material comfort one quickly gets used to.

In politics, money is a sensitive subject. Parties have funds, but their use is strictly regulated and sometimes open to interpretation. It is not uncommon for a party to try to partially offset the loss of income of those who commit themselves full-time. This is an accepted practice when it follows the rules, yet it remains surrounded by ambiguities. In my case, that compensation covered only a portion of what I had left behind. I accepted this reality: serving a political cause also meant earning less.

Two weeks later, Lucien Paiement came to meet the mayor after his defeat. I have always compared politics to boxing.

The boxer becomes world champion. He raises the belt; the crowd cheers. He trains for months to defend his title. He is confident of winning again. Surrounded by his team, he steps into the ring. But once the bell rings, he is alone. The crowd shouts his name. In the second round, a fatal blow. He collapses. He loses. He hands over his belt in front of 20,000 people. He gets up and shakes the winner's hand. The crowd has already dispersed. He has only two choices: start over from scratch... or go home. In his mind, everything collapsed in one evening. The ego takes a hit.

Politics is the same.

The mayor is running for a third term. Eight years of hard work for his city. A great campaign. He is confident. His opponent does not seem up to par. But on election night, he loses. No more power. No more adrenaline. People move away, and officials already turn to the winner. The blow is hard.

The next day, he empties his office. He says goodbye to his employees. A week later, he returns, forced to meet the new mayor. He takes the opportunity to visit Achille and me.

— It's like I was hit by a train, he told us.

We were moved, unable to say a word. That is politics: one day, you're king. The next day, you're dethroned. One day, you have a thousand friends. Next, you are alone. So-called loyalists and officials follow power. That's political ingratitude.

Now part of the executive, I didn't hesitate to prioritize my district, Saint-François. The first thing I did was expropriate the eastern tip of the island to turn it into a park. One must remember that the settlement of Île Jésus—today known as Île de Laval—began in 1672 from its eastern tip. This immense island, bordered by the Rivière des Prairies to the south and the Rivière des Mille Îles to the north, was long seen as fertile and strategic. During New France, King Louis XIV granted seigneuries to encourage colonization. Settlers from Montreal and the St. Lawrence Valley were the first to settle, often near the shoreline for easier access.

This reminder is not trivial. Understanding the roots of a place is also to better grasp the evolution of its power, its institutions, and those who governed—or tried to. Laval, first a rural territory, would become, over time, a playground for political ambitions, economic interests, and sometimes...the excesses of power.

Laval envisioned the east as a large industrial park. BASF was already there, and Stablex wanted in. But I envisioned the east of Laval as agricultural. Thus, in the new 1983 planning scheme, I declared that most of my district should be agricultural. I saw it, surrounded by two rivers, as a large agricultural garden. Living in Saint-François was living in the countryside. I had the entire industrial zone removed. The only plant there was BASF, which decided to leave, and I prevented Stablex from settling.

I also worked on the expropriation of the Riverside Speedway racetrack, which disappeared. For years, I had dreamed of building an arena in Saint-François, but I was always told the population was too small. I had an arena built in Parc du Moulin. The population dreamed of a bridge in the east. We prepared a plan to expropriate land to link Lévesque Boulevard to Montée Masson, a route that would one day serve the future bridge and, for now, help residents reach Pie IX Bridge without passing through Saint-Vincent-de-Paul. The bridge was later built exactly where the road had been expropriated.

This fracture between my ideal and reality sowed a deep doubt in me. I had dreamed of wielding power to transform the city, improve lives, and make a difference. But what I discovered was the slowness of the machine, backroom dealings, power struggles, and promises diluted in delays or compromise.

The parallel power still existed. The infamous "ring." That network of influence is composed of fundraisers, entrepreneurs, and developers. Skilled, elegant, and charming, they invited me to their luxurious villas. I refused.

Because I knew that behind their smiles was an unspoken deal. Their hospitality had a price: my loyalty.

Claude went with his friend, the entrepreneur. I resisted. That distance isolated me.

When a young snow removal contractor called me, shaken because an official had asked him for $1,000 to get a contract, I acted. I demanded the official be dismissed. That was my first clear act against the system. And not the last.

At the Laval Transit Corporation, a once-untouchable commissioner, protected by the networks of the time, was forced to leave under my pressure. I also defended a courageous urban planner on the executive who wanted to tackle illegal signage. Despite threats, we held firm. Slowly, we restored some dignity to the city.

But this constant struggle had a cost. I was disturbed. I saw fear in certain eyes. Whispers in hallways. My calls were ignored. I had power, but I was losing something else: lightness, joy, the dream.

I was becoming a solitary man.

Power wears you down. Not only because it demands, but also because it reveals. It exposes our limits, our contradictions, and our illusions. And it forces us to choose:

give in to the comfort of inaction... or face the storms, at the risk of losing oneself.

I had chosen the storm.

Chapter 8: Mulroney's Call

In February 1983, an unexpected call changed my path. Brian Mulroney, then president of Iron Ore, wanted to meet me. Rumor had it that he would be running for the leadership of the Progressive Conservative Party of Canada, led by Joe Clark. Recommended by the president of the Journal de Montréal, his call reached me in the middle of an executive committee meeting. He wanted a meeting.

A week later, I was climbing for the first time the wide stone staircase of the Mount Royal Club, located on Sherbrooke Street West in Montreal. This private club, the oldest in Canada, has a majestic atmosphere. A uniformed concierge welcomed me and led me to a large lounge decorated with old paintings. In a corner, under the windows, was a large table covered with a white cloth, where Brian was already seated. He stood, shook my hand, and invited me to sit.

Warm, tall, and clearly in good shape, he got straight to the point: he believed he had found in me the political organizer he was looking for, a man recognized for his achievements, demonstrated by my current role as vice president of the Laval executive committee. Would I agree to be the chief organizer of his campaign in Quebec? The leadership race was to take place on June 11 in Ottawa. I had four months left.

His proposal electrified me. Managing the city alongside Claude Lefebvre had drained much of my energy. I also knew that organizing a leadership campaign—a first for me—appealed more than managing a city. Without asking for time to think, I immediately agreed to collaborate.

At my age, I saw it as a great challenge, a chance for recognition, and the opportunity to step beyond Laval, which I had already fully explored. For the next four months, I served the city from 8 a.m. to noon, then worked on Brian Mulroney's campaign in Quebec from 1 p.m. until late at night.

A week later, during a large gathering of friends and supporters at the Queen Elizabeth Hotel, Brian Mulroney officially announced his candidacy and introduced those who would lead him to victory. I was, of course, among them. There was also Pierre Péladeau, hockey player Bobby Orr, some provincial premiers, and about a hundred other personalities and business people from across Canada supporting him.

Being a "man of the people" and wanting to stay that way, I felt uncomfortable among celebrities, but I forced myself and shook hands. The next day and throughout the week, the newspapers covered my entry onto the federal stage.

I now had to contribute to Mulroney's victory by winning over as many delegates from Quebec—and even Canada—as possible. Over the following three months, I traveled across parts of Quebec and met most of the leaders of the 75 electoral ridings to encourage them to support Brian. I went as far as Toronto and Winnipeg to urge business people to support Brian and influence the delegates attending the leadership convention.

I realized that, in a leadership race, money is also the lifeblood. To elect delegates in the ridings, it wasn't enough to count on Conservatives. The organization filled halls with all kinds of people who paid to vote for the delegates.

I understood then that he had approached me not for my organizational skills, but for my image and notoriety as someone who had achieved the impossible by defeating Paiement in Laval. He didn't need an organizer; he needed a politically recognized figure in Quebec. I recalled the gathering at Queen Elizabeth: most attendees were well-known personalities. I wasn't that type of person. I was a man who liked to take on challenges—once accomplished, I moved on.

I had never imagined how many people in Laval wanted to see me fail. I would soon find out; as soon as I began forming my team, my old adversaries turned against me, fighting against Mulroney. Nearly 500 people attended the delegate convention in my Duvernay riding. In each riding, delegates were elected to attend the June 11 leadership convention in Ottawa. National newspapers and television were focused on me. Nearly all the delegates from my riding sided with Joe Clark.

I had to make sure my disappointment didn't show. My response to the media was:

— Duvernay was a tough battle and a good experience.

We lost a fight, not the war, and I was convinced Brian Mulroney would be the new Conservative leader. After hearing me on television, Brian called to say he appreciated the comment, saying it was fair.

Journalists weren't fooled, and the next day's headlines read:

BUSSEY, MULRONEY'S ORGANIZER IN QUEBEC, LOSSES NEARLY ALL DELEGATES IN HIS OWN RIDING.

What a blow! The slap I had just received reflected Paiement's election and my old colleagues' losses. That night, I realized I had many enemies.

Brian absolutely needed Quebec to win the leadership, and I was convinced the race would come down to Mulroney and Clark. Three days before the final date, Saturday, June 11, 1983, Mulroney's team was buzzing with activity in Ottawa. It was about capturing the undecided votes. More than half of Quebec's delegates had already pledged support to Brian. Most were staying in hotels in Hull (Gatineau), where I also stayed, even though Brian wanted me in Ottawa.

To win over the undecided and those leaning against him, we had set up a recruitment team to court delegates during the three evenings held in Hull and Ottawa. That's when I understood there was also a network of dozens of "back men" collecting money across Canada. Delegates had to be treated well.

Around 9 a.m. Saturday morning, the delegates began arriving at the Ottawa Centre. Radio, television, and print journalists were out in force. Organizers and their teams moved through the hall to get a view of the zones assigned to each candidate. Delegates were easily recognizable, wearing shirts or scarves in their candidate's colors.

After each round, we had to lobby on the floor for our candidate, trying to persuade delegates whose candidate had been eliminated to switch to Brian. Late in the evening, after several rounds, Brian was elected leader of the Conservative Party. Around midnight, I returned to Laval, mission accomplished, but disappointed with my experience. The next morning, I received a call from Brian Mulroney inviting me to the grand reception he was hosting in Ottawa for his collaborators. I declined, citing municipal files, but the real reason was that I didn't feel aligned with some of the people whose thirst for power I had seen. Canada was vast, and power here was quite different from city politics. I needed distance.

On August 29, 1983, Brian Mulroney was elected MP in a by-election in Central Nova, New Brunswick. I attended his swearing-in in Ottawa. He insisted:

— Ronald, you must absolutely run in Laval. You'd make a good minister.

He was offering me power. Was it to reward me for my unpaid work on his campaign? I said I needed to think.

At 38, vice president of Laval's executive, having represented Brian Mulroney in Quebec—now leader of the Conservative Party of Canada—I felt unhappy. I thought politics had worn me out. But at the time, I also thought I didn't know how to do anything else. I saw no new challenge in politics.

Even for a political enthusiast—what comes next? You can leave politics, but politics doesn't leave you. People often see older politicians as at the end of their careers, but I was young when I saw it up close. It's all-consuming, all the satisfaction it brings. It blinds you. You think there's nothing else to replace it.

I was on a power trip.

Chapter 9: Betrayal

Municipal politics had ceased to be a challenge for me well before I ventured into federal politics. I found myself at an internal impasse. Upon returning to City Hall, everything felt routine, déjà vu. Nothing stimulated me anymore. Yet, I had no intention of running in Laval East, but the shadow of Brian Mulroney, the opportunities he embodied, and the emerging federal ambitions—all of it drew me in. Still impulsive, I assembled a small organization. An informal poll revealed that my candidacy would resonate strongly. It was flattering. It made me feel alive again.

But alongside that, a deep fear settled in.

What if I left and became nothing?

We dedicate years to politics, to serving, battling, and building credibility. But we often forget to consider what comes after. What do we do when we're no longer "councilors," "the mayor's right-hand man," or the one consulted before signing a contract?

Nothing.

Silence.

Emptiness.

Anonymity.

I was 39 years old. I had known only three real jobs: Household Finance, Wyeth, and the city. I owned a residence for the elderly, so I was financially free. But internally, I wasn't. Politics had shaped me. It had fed my desires, my need for recognition, and my quest for impact.

When Claude offered me, during the holidays, the idea of "bequeathing" me the mayoralty, it shook me. The man in me sensed a scam, a maneuver. But the dreamer, the ambitious one, the child from Verdun who wanted to make history... he listened.

For weeks, I pretended to consider it. The truth? I couldn't silence my ego.

Becoming mayor? That would be the pinnacle.

I didn't listen to my instincts.

They told me to run.

They screamed that it wasn't my path.

But I couldn't follow them.

After the holidays, I responded positively to Claude Lefebvre. At the February caucus, he announced to the entire team that he wouldn't seek re-election and wished to hand over his position to me. I was already doing the work, collaborating with the councilors, and they all agreed.

I called Brian to tell him I was staying in Laval, assuring him that Laval East would be secured for him. In my mind, I had found a new "job," but in reality, I was merely changing chairs. I didn't concern myself with what the entrepreneur and the "sharks" thought.

In May, Claude invited me to dinner with his close friend, an engineer at an engineering firm in Laval. He announced that he had changed his mind, under pressure from his friends, and proposed that I stay for another term with him.

My response was immediate:

— No, you can't do that.

I had declined Brian Mulroney's offer. I was no longer interested in managing the city. What I didn't know was that the engineer friend had a Plan B: Gilles Vaillancourt.

The influencers of the "system," under Paiement's guidance, had chosen Vaillancourt to take the reins. They met with Claude Lefebvre to convince him to dismiss me from the executive committee, orchestrating a coup despite the support he had shown me in front of all the PRO councilors.

On June 22, at six in the morning, the phone rang. Nicole Giasson, the party secretary, invited me to read La Presse. On the front page:

COUP IN LAVAL: LEFEBVRE DISMISSES BUSSEY AND CORBO

The shock was brutal. Claude had dismissed two members of the executive committee. Everything was false. The system didn't want me as mayor. They preferred Vaillancourt: more docile, more compliant.

This betrayal struck me to the core. Claude had fired me. Without discussion. Without a glance.

A journalist held more power over my life than I did. More influence over my public image than I could ever hope to claim for myself. Three words on the front page of La Presse that Friday morning—and my world came crashing down. I felt paralyzed, helpless. The press, which knew me all too well, had been given orders to publish without contacting me, without hearing my side of the story. It was Saint-Jean-Baptiste weekend. The timing felt deliberate, calculated to leave me defenseless. Once the false story was released, the doubt had already taken hold. It crept into every look, every whisper, every silence. And me? I was left standing alone, asking myself: how do you fight back when the verdict has already been delivered? How do you rebuild when the damage is already done?

I sat on the edge of the bed, newspaper in hand, heart emptied.

Eleven years.

Annihilated.

No defense.

No explanation.

Just the brutality of the system.

In the following days, I was overwhelmed by a mix of rage, sadness, and incomprehension.

Why me?

Why now?

Why so cowardly?

But deep down, I knew.

I was disruptive.

I wasn't pliable.

I didn't compromise with fundraisers or engineers close to power.

The system needed Vaillancourt. I had become an obstacle.

Objective achieved, Claude brought Vaillancourt into the executive to lead the city. Then he resigned in June 1989, citing health reasons.

Vaillancourt took over the PRO, a party born for citizen consultation, but now derailed. After 33 years in power, this old Laval party was manipulated by two mayors. In 2013, Vaillancourt resigned under the weight of corruption and gangsterism allegations. He ended up in prison. The system collapsed.

Claude, meanwhile, had become wealthy.

I could have written a book about the political system. But it would have brought me no pleasure.

Power in politics is a thin line between good and evil.

Today, I believe that period was necessary.

It prepared the ground for new desires.

I have named very few people in this book. That's intentional.

My goal in sharing this political journey is to show that the impossible is possible.

At 39, despite the failure, I still believed in the future. But I needed to heal and learn an essential lesson:

What I don't control makes me vulnerable and leads me to make poor decisions.

In the future, I must take control in risky moments.

And wounded pride is a poor advisor.

It was in this inner chaos that I made the most difficult decision of my life: to resign.

Not out of weakness.

Not out of abandonment.

But to find myself again. To become a free man once more.

I didn't know what the future held. But I knew one thing:

I could no longer live in this mire.

That decision saved me.

It paved the way for a new life.

I learned that power can devour and that ambition can distort.

But falling isn't failing.

Sometimes, it's the only path to the light.

After my resignation, I had to relearn everything: to breathe differently, to get up without a mandate, and to live without being accountable to anyone. For months, I felt suspended between two worlds—the one I had just left with a bang and the one I didn't yet know. I was no longer a politician. I wasn't yet something else. It was in that void that the rebirth began. It came to me. Then that's a word: dare.

Chapter 10: DARE: Rebuilding

Accepting defeat is hard. But getting back up... that requires much more than courage. It demands an inner strength we didn't know we had. It means daring to look life in the face, without a mask, without pretenses.

For years, I gave everything to politics. Body, soul, convictions. I left a part of myself there. And after the betrayal, a void settled in. That void where nothing seems to make sense anymore. Where each day resembles the last, with no clear direction.

But I transformed that void into a space for rebirth.

I had to relearn everything. Breathe differently. Wake up in the morning with no mandate. Live without being accountable. Learn to exist—not as an elected official or a decision-maker, but as a free man.

I was no longer a politician.

But I wasn't yet something else.

It was in that suspended moment that the rebuilding began.

Step by step.

Without plans.

Without certainties.

But with a desire to return to what really matters.

I found pleasure again in simple things: a walk in the woods, a meal with friends, and a sincere gaze. I reconnected with what I had neglected. With my deep desires, my values. I understood I didn't need a title to exist. It's not the position that gives value to a man. It's the man who gives meaning to what he does.

I dared to reinvent myself.

To dare is to be afraid, but to move forward anyway.

It is decided that the fall will not be the end, but a starting point.

I began to dream differently. Not of power anymore, but of projects that reflected who I was. I opened new doors. I returned to entrepreneurship, to real estate, to activities where I could build and create without denying who I was.

This desert crossing taught me one thing: there is no real freedom without alignment between what we think, what we say, and what we do.

The day I accepted not to please everyone, I began to please myself.

The day I stopped wanting to prove, I began to be.

The day I realized I had nothing to lose, I discovered everything was to gain.

This chapter of my life—I didn't choose it.

But I went through it.

And more importantly, I transformed it.

The keyword of this turning point is *dare*.

Dare to leave a comfortable position.
Dare to face your wounds.
Dare to build differently.

Because behind every fall lies a possibility.

And behind every scar, a new strength.

When I finally turned the page, it took two full years for the wound to heal—but not the scar.

Those two years were the quietest, the emptiest, and the most defining of my life. For the first time since I was twenty-eight, I had no title, no mandate, and no full schedule. I no longer had to convince, govern, or fight political opponents. In the morning, I woke up with no urgency. And this absence of noise first brought anxiety. Who was I without politics?

Seeing Lefebvre and Vaillancourt running Laval, hearing about Mulroney becoming Prime Minister... all of it rekindled a certain bitterness. I felt betrayed, excluded, and forgotten. And yet, in hindsight, that sidelining was a blessing in disguise.

Stripped of what had driven me for fifteen years, I had to rebuild. And above all, I made myself a promise: never to depend on others again, nor work for anyone else. I still had the drive to build, but this time, it would be for me.

Despite many jobs, I refused them all. The idea of becoming an employee again had become unbearable. I wanted to breathe, to think, to create differently. I first had to understand what had happened to me. So I started writing, like beginning therapy. I wanted to tell the truth about my political experience—not to settle scores, but to understand.

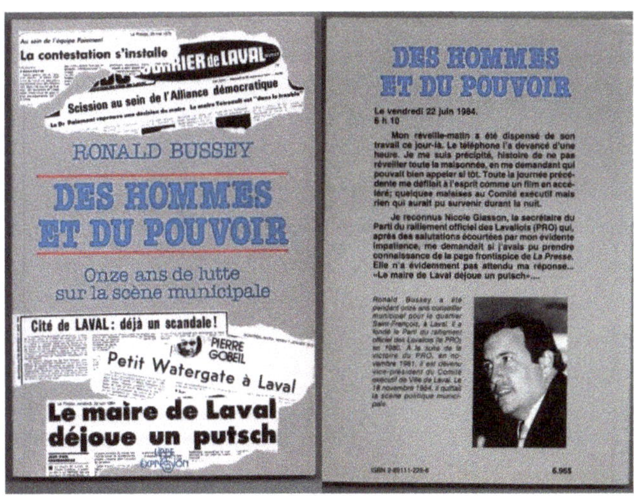

This introspective work was demanding. I relived every disappointment, every betrayal, and every hope, too. I wrote in anger, with clarity, and sometimes in pain. But most of all, I wrote to grieve. My book, Men and Power: Eleven Years of Struggle on the Municipal Stage, published by Libre Expression in 1985, resonated. Nearly two thousand copies were sold. I was invited on the radio, TV, and in the press. People wanted to understand what I had lived through. And I was beginning to understand that my future would never be the same.

Many then suggested I return to politics to challenge Lefebvre in November 1985. I would have had the wind in my sails. But my answer was no. Definitely no. I had turned the page. I needed something else.

I dreamed of a calmer, freer life. Of travel. Of projects without parties, without promises to make, without knives in the back. In December 1984, I decided to leave Laval for good. I sold my condo and moved into my house in Sainte-Adèle. Every time I drove on Highway 15 and reached the "Porte du Nord," I breathed easier. The mountains were ahead of me, and the city behind.

To mark this renewal, I offered my family a trip to Europe for the holidays. Skiing, rest, snow. But also, an unforgettable event: an avalanche. As we climbed toward the Aiguille peak, an avalanche broke loose nearby. Helicopters, search dogs, rescuers... a movie-worthy scene. It was a shock. But it was also a lesson: life can tip over at any moment. So you might as well dare.

Because to dare is to give yourself permission to start over. To try a new life. Not to be defined by what you were, but by what you choose to become.

Chapter 11: Traveling During My Two-Year Semi-Retirement

Working on CN trains during my studies introduced me to travel. I crossed Canada from east to west, gaining a great deal of independence and self-confidence. I loved the adventure. Traveling, for me, is a form of liberation. Taking risks in life, setting off, lifts the pressure from within me. I feel immense freedom, as if I were living another life. The return to daily reality is always difficult. I would later find myself dreaming of continuing my travels and living differently.

In my thirties, every winter, I spent two weeks in different Club Meds in the Caribbean. One year, we visited two clubs: one week in Guadeloupe and one in Martinique. I did a lot of scuba diving, but a night dive in Martinique was an incredible experience.

Around 9 p.m., we boarded a boat. Offshore, a few people were equipped with flashlights. One of the G.O.s informed us that there were 15 feet of water, and we needed to let ourselves sink to the bottom and wait for his signal before turning on our lights. As we descended, we could only see a hazy shadow. Once at the bottom, we waited for the signal. Then, suddenly, a sound from a tank was heard, and hundreds of fish appeared around us. The guide signaled us to rub our bare arms, and suddenly, thousands of tiny lights, like diamonds, rose to the surface. It was magical.

For my second trip to Europe, I wanted to visit as many French and Italian cities as possible in 15 days. From one marvel to the next, I visited Paris, rented a small Renault, and headed for the French Riviera: Monaco, Marseille, the Italian Riviera, Pisa, Geneva, and many other places. We slept in historic hotels and castles, with rooms adorned with majestic wardrobes and canopy beds. We stayed in a Relais & Châteaux property. In Monaco, we booked a room in a hotel next to the casino.

Monaco – The Circus and Chance

Monaco has always fascinated me. This tiny principality, nestled between sea and mountains, embodies luxury, tradition, and precision. Everything seems orchestrated, choreographed, like a grand stage. It was in this fairy-tale setting that I learned the Monte Carlo circus, one of the most prestigious in the world, was performing in town.

This circus is not just entertainment: it's a Monegasque institution, founded in 1974 by Prince Rainier III himself, a great lover of circus arts. Every year, it attracts the world's top performers, judged by a panel presided over by the royal family. It's the elite of the global circus scene, a competition as noble as it is spectacular, in other words: an event not to be missed.

Motivated, I immediately tried to buy tickets. I was told everything had been sold out for months. Nothing could be done, in principle. But I don't give up easily. All my life, I've faced closed doors, refusals, and obstacles. And all my life, I've learned that behind every "no," there is often a possible detour. You just have to find it.

On the evening of the show, I went to the Fontvieille big top anyway, an impressive structure set up a few steps from the port, at the western end of the principality. An elegant crowd, in gowns and tuxedos, filled the area in a hushed excitement. In jeans and sweaters, my companion and I stood out. And yet, I had a feeling something would happen.

I walked up to the ticket booth, ready to try my luck. Moments later, a miracle occurred: a man, clearly unable to attend, came to request a refund for two tickets. Without hesitation, I bought them on the spot. Fourth row, center ring. Dream seats. Thank you, life; thank you, universe.

Just before the show began, the entire audience stood up. A chill ran through the crowd. I didn't understand until I saw Prince Rainier, surrounded by his guests, enter and sit a few rows in front of us. His presence underscored the seriousness of the moment: that evening, he was personally judging the performances. This was not just a show but a celebration of excellence, art, and transcendence.

And what a show it was! Trapeze artists, acrobats, trained horses, poetic clowns... Each act was a technical and artistic feat, executed with the precision of the world's greatest stages. That night, in Monaco, under a starry big top, I was no longer a traveling spectator—I was a child full of wonder, a man fulfilled for having listened to his instincts.

While driving through Geneva, I remembered the restaurant Le Chat-Botté, often mentioned in travel stories. Did it still exist? I stopped the car and asked for directions. "Of course, sir, it's the restaurant of the Beau-Rivage Hotel." Keep straight ahead, it's just over a kilometer from here. This hotel, one of the most renowned in Europe, gave us a room with a view of Lake Geneva. The concierge, surprised, handed us the key and ordered the valet, "Go park the

Canadians' little Renault." What a room! The bathroom floor and towel racks were heated. We rented a movie, and the concierge came to install the player in our room. Unfortunately, the famous restaurant was closed, but we admired its luxurious dining room.

This trip was just an appetizer. It made me want to return and explore more deeply what we had only glimpsed: Pisa, the French Riviera, Marseille. I would return to Italy, France, and beyond.

Diving Trip

A friend who owned a dive shop was organizing a trip for a group of young people. I decided to join them. We arrived in Tel Aviv, a white city under a blue sky. We spent the first day exploring it. The next day, we boarded a boat for three days of diving, with two sessions per day and lunch on board, before returning to sleep at the hotel. The water was exceptionally clear, very calm, and teeming with an incredible variety of colorful fish.

Then we spent two days near the Dead Sea, where we swam in very salty water. We covered ourselves in black mud, let it dry in the sun, then rinsed off in the sea—an ideal treatment for the skin.

Next, we crossed the border into Egypt by bus to reach Mount Sinai. The stop in the middle of the desert was memorable: no restaurant, just a green "giblotte" served on plates that only one of us dared to eat. I opted instead to buy pita bread from a lady baking flatbreads over an open fire. Fortunately, I had my jar of peanut butter—a travel habit that often came in handy.

After a night in a questionable hotel, we dove for two more days in the Red Sea, a warm and very salty body of water. The seabed was spectacular, filled with fish and corals reminiscent of Chinese gardens.

I left the group for a few days. The most striking incident of the trip occurred when a rock shattered our car's rear window while driving through Ramallah during a riot.

Extremely nervous, I sped toward Jerusalem, where we changed vehicles before beginning a pilgrimage to the Wailing Wall, the 14 Stations of the Cross, and the Garden of Gethsemane. The trip ended in Bethlehem, where we visited the Church of the Nativity before rejoining our group in Tel Aviv for the return to Montreal.

Fulfilling My Parents' Dream

My mother's dream had always been to see Paris. In the spring of 1991, I decided to give my parents that gift: fourteen unforgettable days in France, just the three of us. I wanted to show them everything, as if every moment had to engrave the intensity of this journey into our memories.

Of course, the first stop was the Eiffel Tower, followed by a panoramic bus tour to Versailles, then a cruise on the Seine to admire the City of Light in all its splendor. We continued to Strasbourg, exploring Alsatian vineyards together, and since they loved games and betting, I treated them to a magical evening at the Royal Casino of Évian-les-Bains.

My father, supposed to be my co-pilot, would fold the map as soon as he opened it, preferring to admire the scenery rather than read the roads. That trip, which they called the most beautiful of their lives, revealed to me the strength of a couple bound by decades of love and complicity. Even today, knowing that I was able to give them the realization of that dream fills me with deep happiness.

Motorhome to Mexico

In Sainte-Adèle, I bought a motorhome, which allowed me to travel everywhere: Canada, the United States, and Mexico. I realized it was the ideal way to travel. We left in mid-January, heading toward Louisiana, New Orleans, Houston, then San Antonio—a romantic city with its canal. We continued to El Paso, where we crossed the Mexican border to reach Chihuahua, Pancho Villa's city, then headed to Copper Canyon.

We loaded our 30-foot motorhome onto a freight train. I noticed railroad ties were placed under the front and rear wheels, secured with chains. I quickly understood their purpose when the train started. For the two nights and three days of travel, we lived in our motorhome. From the moment the train departed, the vehicle began to sway violently. I was convinced it would dislocate or derail. Sitting in the front during the day, the view was terrifying, especially around curves.

At the first stop, I got out to inspect the motorhome. Everything seemed intact. I spoke with a train employee, who assured me there was no danger and that the night would be easier since we wouldn't see the train's motion.

The first day was the hardest, but by nightfall, the view was sublime: a starry sky with no light pollution. It felt like we were traveling toward the heavens, deep in the canyon. Arriving in Los Mochis, we spent a night before boarding a ferry to La Paz, where we stayed five days in Baja California. We also spent two days in Loreto, on the Gulf of Mexico.

On the way back, we passed through San Diego, stopped in Palm Springs to enjoy the mineral pools, and then spent four days in Las Vegas at the Circus Circus Hotel campground. Then on to Los Angeles, up Route 1 to San Francisco and its vineyards. Three months after our departure, we were back in mid-April.

We repeated the experience for several winters, often returning to Mexico, to our campsite by the Caribbean—a little paradise where we met travelers from all over.

Those two years of travel transformed me.

They were much more than a break: they were a rebirth. I had set off to escape myself, but ended up finding myself. Every landscape crossed, every culture encountered, every silence shared with the sea or the mountains left a mark.

I had learned to live differently.

More freely. More lightly. More presently.

But deep inside, something was still stirring.

Not the desire to go back.

Rather, the call of a new challenge.

One morning, waking up with my eyes lost in the mountains of Sainte-Adèle, I said to myself,

"And now, what do I build?"

That was the beginning of a new adventure.

PART TWO
MY SECOND LIFE

Since the beginning of this book, I've been telling the story of my journey: politics, battles, projects, victories...

I've asked myself more than once:

Am I talking too much about myself? Do I sound like I'm boasting?

Honestly… I don't want to. I'm not writing this book to flatter my ego or build myself a statue.

I'm writing it because I believe it can be useful. Because if I, a guy from Verdun, was able to realize my dreams, then others can too.

But to explain how I did it, I have to talk about myself.

Because I want to show a path—my path. With its successes, its mistakes, and its doubts as well.

I haven't always been right. I've made bad choices. I've experienced failures. But I've always moved forward with ideas, energy, instinct, and, above all, a desire to build—to change things.

This book isn't about shining. It's about passing something on.

Passing something on to those who want to start something, dare, and step outside the box. To those who want to do something with their lives, even if they weren't dealt the best cards to begin with.

I talk about politics because I believe it is a tool to make a difference.

I talk about my business ventures because I wanted to create, invest, and transform places no one saw potential in.

I talk about travel because I discovered, later in life, what it truly means to be free.

So now, what you're about to read, in this second part, is my second life:

The one where I changed direction, followed new passions, and took new risks.

Because success isn't just about reaching the top.

It's about continuing to move forward, to create, to inspire.

Chapter 12: Rebuilding with Passion

After we moved to Sainte-Adèle, between our travels, I decided to take a real estate course—not to become an agent, but to better understand the housing and commercial property market, as well as property evaluation. For eight weeks, at Cégep Montmorency in Laval, I completed this course and obtained my real estate agent's license, though I never used it. However, I had a feeling this knowledge would be useful in the future, even if I didn't yet know how.

One day, as I wandered through the village of Saint-Sauveur, its main street lined with cafés, upscale restaurants, and boutiques, enchanted me. This village made me dream. In 1985, Tremblant had not yet been developed, and Saint-Sauveur attracted Montreal's jet set. Charming, like a postcard, this place inspired me. I found myself thinking:

I'd like to do business here. This village seems prosperous.

A few days after saying those words, my real estate agent—the same one who found our property in Sainte-Adèle—contacted me with an interesting offer: the purchase of a three-story building located across from the church in Saint-Sauveur, on the main street. This 10,000-square-foot, century-old building had a Chinese restaurant, a bar, and a nightclub on its two main floors. My agent, Philippe, who was working with a restaurateur, was looking for a third partner to turn the place into a small indoor shopping center, where the current owner would retain a bar. It was love at first sight. We partnered equally, and, unable to delegate the management of my ventures, I enthusiastically took on the project. Finally, a new challenge—and since I was used to solving problems and taking risks, I was passionate about this adventure.

As I provided the necessary guarantees, we secured a loan from the Federal Business Development Bank. However, an unexpected twist almost delayed the transaction: when it came time to sign the deed of sale, the owner seriously hesitated. But I was about to leave for India and didn't want to postpone my trip. A meeting was arranged between the owner, my lawyer, and me.

Meanwhile, Francine, my wife, had a dream: India. I was about to leave for India and couldn't postpone the trip. A meeting was set with my lawyer. The negotiations dragged on, but just before boarding the plane, my phone rang: the transaction was finalized. Joy overwhelmed me. I knew this project would be a success.

As the discussion dragged on, I had to leave, so I gave my lawyer power of attorney. Just before boarding the plane, she called to tell me the deal was done. I was overjoyed! I was certain this purchase would be a success.

We arrived in New Delhi, and an intense feeling of disorientation washed over us: another world, unimaginable poverty alongside incredible wealth. We were always accompanied by a different guide in each city, staying in five-star hotels. One day, I asked one of our guides why people, despite their lack of education and extreme poverty, always seemed happy. He answered by telling me his story:

"I was born in the mountains and grew up in a cave—no radio, no television, no newspaper, no car, not even a bicycle. We lived as a family, cut off from the world, but we were happy. One day, I left the mountain for New Delhi, where I slept on the street like so many others. I found a job, then managed to rent a room. I saw my neighbor's bicycle and wanted one too. Remember this: what you don't know and what you don't see doesn't awaken desire in you. The problem begins when you start to want things. That's when

life gets complicated, because you begin to envy your neighbor."

He pointed to the passersby and added,

— Look at them. They're happy, content with what they have.

This story powerfully illustrates how desire is born through social comparison. As long as we don't see what others possess, we don't desire it. It's a fundamental truth: our desires are often shaped by what we perceive around us, not by our actual needs. Happiness seems more tied to contentment than to possession.

But this raises an interesting tension with the theme of My Dreams, My Desires. Because dreaming is also about envisioning more, wanting better, aspiring higher. If we follow the man from the mountains, desire becomes a source of trouble. Yet without desire, there's no transformation, no self-actualization.

We continued our journey to Agra to admire the Taj Mahal, which we first glimpsed from afar, beyond a gate leading to a garden and a walkway nearly a thousand feet long. Breathless before this masterpiece, we took in the sight of this mausoleum built between 1631 and 1645 by the Mughal emperor Shah Jahan in tribute to his beloved wife.

Made of white marble, it is one of the Seven Wonders of the World. The emperor had planned to build a second Taj Mahal in black marble across the river, but he died in 1666 before realizing his dream.

Taj Mahal

The next day, we saw the Ganges at six in the morning. Around our boat floated human bones, while bodies burned on the shore. The scene was overwhelming. Despite this, worshippers continued to bathe in the sacred river, following their belief. Later, we wandered through streets crowded with cows, elephants, and dogs, where men got haircuts or relieved themselves in the shadow of a wall. The contrast was striking with a beautiful blooming garden where we had lunch, enjoying absolute peace and a heady fragrance.

Our journey continued in Nepal with a photo safari in the heart of the jungle. Staying at Tiger Tops Tharu, a lodge of extreme comfort, we had the chance to see rhinos racing by—a breathtaking sight where the ground shook beneath their feet. On the second night, we slept in a tent, hoping to see tigers. It was so cold we thought we'd freeze, but hot water bottles placed under our mattresses allowed us to sleep peacefully. The next morning, we discovered paw prints proving the tigers had circled our camp overnight.

We then stayed on an island facing Tibet. To reach our hotel, we crossed a river on a raft pulled by ropes. Before dinner, we navigated near Tibet, where we saw an old man playing the flute, alone on a rock, in absolute silence. The next day at dawn, we watched the sunrise reflected on a lake—a scene of calming beauty.

Our journey ended in Sri Lanka, where we spent two days on a houseboat. A personal cook prepared our meals, and a servant came every morning to light a wood stove to warm us. In autumn, locals wore long tunics and carried wooden bowls filled with burning leaves to warm themselves with the smoke. Throughout this extraordinary journey, we took about a dozen flights, sometimes landing in cow fields or boarding with a simple wooden staircase.

When we returned from Asia, something in me had changed. The man of projects, always seeking action, came back with a broader, calmer vision. This journey had awakened my senses, shaken my certainties, and rekindled my creative spirit. I had seen beauty in simplicity, humanity in chaos.

Chapter 13: Create, Surround Yourself, Build

Back in Quebec, I went to study the Faubourg Sainte-Catherine, near Guy Street in Montreal, where old stables had been transformed into the base for a new kind of indoor shopping center. Numerous small boutiques and ethnic restaurants were arranged around the ground-floor agora and a mezzanine, creating a sense of grandeur that struck me as ideal for my Saint-Sauveur project.

I called on the designer who had conceived the Faubourg Sainte-Catherine in Montreal. Exceptionally talented, he would become a friend and a constant collaborator. The plan he produced required the removal of the Chinese restaurant and a complete transformation of the existing building, starting with the creation of two shops in the basement.

From there, customers could access the parking lot and the ground-floor premises via a wide, elegant staircase. Another suspended staircase would lead to the upper floor, where other shops and offices would be located. The facade, facing the main street, would blend harmoniously with the village while providing access to the eight ground-floor businesses.

The work required a significant investment. The loan to proceed was based on projected rental income. The center's name was obvious: it would be called Faubourg Saint-Sauveur.

After years of proving myself, the idea of taking a new direction imposed itself on me. An ambitious project began to take shape in my mind: to transform a mundane space into a vibrant, warm, and attractive indoor shopping center.

Rather than just a commercial space, we wanted to create a place for living. We envisioned a bright space with wide aisles, elegant displays, and relaxing areas where people could stroll. The materials had to reflect quality: wood, glass, and soft lighting. We bet on creating a more human ambiance. This project wasn't just a business venture. It was a builder's dream—a way to prove that profit and beauty could coexist, that commerce could also be a place of connection, even culture.

Every morning, I woke up with renewed energy. Seeing the skeleton of the building take shape, choosing the details, convincing merchants to join the adventure... It was all invigorating. A project like this isn't driven by numbers but by heart.

Few people believed the project was feasible. Turning a 100-year-old building into a shopping center seemed foolish to many. At that time, I was still recovering, physically and emotionally weakened by the recent challenges of my political past. Predictions of failure came from all sides: Too risky, you'll lose your shit. These external voices tried to sow doubt, and sometimes, I heard them too loudly. But deep down, a conviction carried me. I couldn't explain why, but I saw what others didn't yet see. I held onto that vision with stubborn energy. To protect myself, I learned to distinguish between well-founded criticism and fear-driven opinions. I cultivated my confidence by surrounding myself with a few allies who also believed in the dream, and above all, by fueling it daily with action.

January 1986: the Faubourg's walls still echoed with the past, but I was already walking through its reimagined corridors. The opening was scheduled for August. Nothing would derail me.

I started looking for tenants with my plans and a rental pricing chart. Nothing had been built yet, but my pitch was convincing enough that after only three weeks, I secured a lease with A.-L. Van Houte Cafés.

The presence of this prestigious tenant made subsequent negotiations easier. The owners of "Dans un-Jardin" also signed on for a storefront location. The La Capitale real estate agency committed to 1,500 square feet on the second floor and a smaller space on the ground floor.

While still looking for tenants, my partners told me they had found a buyer whose offer would make us all money. But I was enjoying the project too much to just flip it. I had become the old Ronald again: bold, confident, and above all, passionate. Instead of selling, I offered to buy out their shares. They agreed, and I had one month to close the deal.

One Sunday, while at the Faubourg, a man in his forties approached me. He had just bought the neighboring building that housed a bookstore and was eyeing my center. Even though my project wasn't for sale, I was open to discussion. The next day, we had breakfast together. In the end, he invested money in the project, which allowed me to pay off my partners and a line of credit I had used to fund plans and urgent work.

We were now equal partners in the Faubourg, and I owned a third of the bookstore. Our agreement also stated that I would coordinate all expansion work for the Faubourg and the bookstore without compensation.

I accepted a partner I didn't know, betting everything would go well. The deal seemed promising. Together, we secured a loan from Toronto Dominion Bank.

With my plans in hand, I went to City Hall to get my permit. To my surprise, I had to meet with the police chief, who also handled permits. After leading a city like Laval, it was a radical change. The Faubourg, over 100 years old, was designated a heritage site. I was allowed to perform all interior work but had to preserve the external appearance. I got the permit.

I excavated the basement to add two shops. I dismantled the second-floor facade to create a 1,500-square-foot unit. I managed the entire construction, hiring subcontractors. I had succeeded in creating the first small indoor shopping center in the village. All those years working with engineers, architects, and contractors in Laval had proven extremely useful.

I had just discovered what my next job would be: independent entrepreneur, creating and building projects. I realized I could live a semi-retirement, work on projects, and travel.

The official inauguration took place in August 1986, attended by the media, public figures, and local residents. A giant clock topped with the sign "Faubourg Saint-Sauveur" decorated the main entrance.

We wanted the event to reflect who we were: simple, human, warm. The night before, I stayed late, alone in the center. I sat on a wooden bench under the hanging lights and breathed deeply.

The calm before the excitement.

The next morning, from dawn, the crowd began to arrive: families, merchants, the curious. You could feel something special was happening. Children ran from one shop to another, parents enjoyed coffee, and laughter echoed through the halls. The bet had paid off.

A few days later, Michel, owner of a clothing store, told me emotionally:

— Mr. Bussey, I was scared at first. But today, I'm proud. We created something unique. People don't just come to shop—they come to experience something.

Those words echoed in me like confirmation. This center wasn't just a business location; it was a place of belonging.

A living space. A success built on dreams, courage, and the will to do things differently.

All the spaces were rented. On opening day, more than 2,000 people came to visit and shop. Foot traffic was so high that we added a terrace connecting the bookstore and the A.-L. Van Houtte café, uniting the two buildings into one. Saint-Sauveur had its nerve center. As important as the parish church and the popular Pagé bakery. I had created a landmark consistently visited by the jet set, local leaders, and decision-makers.

In May 1987, I explained that real estate had become my top priority.

M. Ronald Bossey est très connu dans les basses Laurentides pour ses activités à titre d'administrateur et d'homme public. Il a déjà occupé le poste de vice-président exécutif du comité exécutif de la Ville de Laval. Âgé de 41 ans, il n'a présentement qu'une seule préoccupation, celle de faire fructifier au maximum ses investissements. Comment? En privilégiant d'emblée le secteur immobilier. «J'ai acquis ma première maison à l'âge de 22 ans. Je l'ai vendue en réalisant un gain de capital fort intéressant pour l'époque. Ensuite, j'en ai acheté une autre que j'ai rapidement revendue en faisant un profit encore plus important. Très tôt, j'ai compris que l'immobilier pouvait être fort rentable.»

M. Bossey s'intéresse au secteur immobilier tant résidentiel que commercial. Ainsi, il aime bien faire l'acquisition de terrains en bordure des avenues importantes de petites municipalités, principalement dans les Laurentides, là où il croit qu'il y aura éventuellement développement. Présentement, il est copropriétaire d'une bâtisse commerciale, le Faubourg Saint-Sauveur, qui abritera une vingtaine de boutiques à partir de juin prochain. Il est aussi copropriétaire d'un centre d'accueil pour personnes âgées. De plus, il possède deux propriétés résidentielles.

Toutes ces activités n'empêchent nullement M. Bossey de diversifier quelque peu son portefeuille. Il gère lui-même son REER en acquérant des obligations à long terme et des actions sûres, celles de compagnies solidement implantées. Par nature, il n'affectionne pas particulièrement les actions comportant un haut degré de risque.

M. Bossey consacre environ cinq heures par semaine à la gestion de ses finances personnelles. Il puise ses sources d'information surtout dans les médias écrits. Pour le reste, il fait entièrement confiance aux professionnels qui l'entourent (comptable, avocat, courtier en valeurs mobilières, etc.) De son propre avis, cette stratégie a toujours su lui apporter les résultats souhaités, «il ne faut surtout pas craindre de faire appel aux services de gens qualifiés», conclut-il.

36 • Affaires + • Mai 1987

Business Review

Two years after building the Faubourg, I thought back to my ski trip in the Alps and had an idea. The rear of the Faubourg's second floor was a huge window with a direct view of the Mont Saint-Sauveur ski slopes.

With the help of my surveyor, we measured the distance from the Faubourg to Mont Saint-Sauveur: about 1 km. We designed a gondola project linking the Faubourg to the ski hill's parking lot, running along rue de la Gare. I contacted companies specializing in such infrastructure and met the village mayor to present my idea. He refused, unable to believe in my ambition, even as I tried to explain the international impact such a project could have.

A few years later, Tremblant completed a similar project: a village with a gondola linking the parking lot to the slopes, crossing roads and hotels. Tremblant has since become an international destination. Once again, my vision was too ahead of its time. Thinking big often unsettles those around us—and I would learn that again in my new life.

When the Faubourg began operating almost on its own, another idea took root in my mind to attract tourists. I contacted the Quebec arts scene to obtain personal items or clothing to display in small glass cases. I created around thirty: Claude Dubois's sneakers, a pipe from Fernand Gignac, the first front page of the Journal de Montréal, a text from Félix Leclerc, and more. Each case featured the item, a photo, and a short explanatory note, installed between shops throughout the center.

On the front of the building, a showcase displayed a dress from Michelle Richard and her father Ti-Blanc Richard's violin. Above the main entrance doors, a sign read:

ARTISTS' ALLEY

Faubourg 1986

Chapter 14: The Land of Séraphin: My Second Project in the Laurentians

After the Faubourg Saint-Sauveur, the desire to create, to build, and to push my limits still lived within me. It wasn't just a need to succeed—it was the pure joy of transforming an idea into reality.

Sainte-Adèle, nestled in the heart of the Laurentians, had long since conquered my heart. This thriving village, once founded by northern pioneers, had become a sought-after vacation destination, cherished both for its mountainous scenery and its cultural vibrancy. Artists, writers, and musicians had settled there over the decades, drawn by the beauty of the surroundings and the inspiration it offered. The Le Chantecler hotel, with its famous lounges, ski slopes, golf course, and social events, added to the charm and reputation of the region.

It was in this setting that a new opportunity presented itself. A friend from Laval offered me a plot of land situated on a mountainside, on the east side of the highway, directly across from our family home. The view was breathtaking:

the ski slopes of Chantecler and the majestic Laurentians in the background.

But there was more than just the landscape. This land had a story. It had once belonged to Séraphin Poudrier, the famous character from Les Pays d'en Haut. For many, this land evoked the mythical television series, with its rural intrigues and memorable figures. It was part of Quebec's collective imagination.

Charmed by the location and inspired by its potential, I decided to invest in it with my friend, sharing it equally. Together, we conceived an ambitious project: a residential complex of 180 condominiums, grouped into clusters of five or six units, each sharing a common pool. The land was divided into 30 lots, planned for development in three phases.

The rugged terrain of the site offered a unique opportunity to enhance the escarpments. Rather than levelling them, I wanted to integrate them into the design. Inspired by the panoramic solarium I had installed in my own home, I had the idea of including a glass enclosure overlooking the mountain in each unit. This became the project's identity: Les Verrières du Hameau.

The site's proximity gave me an advantage: I could monitor the progress of the work daily. The first phase began with the development of Rue du Hameau—sewers, aqueduct, and paving. We financed the municipal infrastructure in collaboration with an engineering firm and later handed it over to the city. It was a heavy investment, made before even laying a single foundation. The financial risk was very real.

But an unexpected economic storm struck: mortgage rates reached a historic high of 21%. The effect on the real estate market was brutal. One year after launching sales, only 11 of the first 13 condos had been sold. Still, we kept our word and built the shared pool for these units.

To ease the pressure, we sold one lot to another developer, who built six new condos there. The rest of Phase 1 was reconfigured into six large lots for single-family homes. These sales allowed us to cover all our expenses and avoid losses.

Later, I bought out my partner's share. I held on to Phases 2 and 3, waiting for the market to recover. A few years later, when the conditions improved, I subdivided the remaining land into 28 large lots of more than 25,000 square feet, all connected to municipal services. I resold them gradually, earning a reasonable profit.

I didn't make a fortune from this project, but I didn't lose anything either. What I gained was the experience of a regional real estate development, a better understanding of cyclical markets, and above all, the satisfaction of having built something beautiful, rooted in local history. The land of Séraphin didn't make me richer, but it enriched my life.

Chapter 15: Factory Outlets

For 25 years, I owned various Class A motorhomes. While traveling in the United States, I often stopped at factory outlets—those shopping centers that grouped major brands like Nike, Polo, and Reebok—at discounted prices. I was fascinated. This model didn't yet exist in Quebec. So, I dreamed. Why not create the equivalent in Saint-Sauveur, a village I knew well, located less than an hour from Montreal?

Saint-Sauveur, with its roughly 7,000 residents, sees its population explode every weekend. Tourists flock there for its ski slopes, festivals, restaurants, and boutiques. It is one of the few Quebec villages that thrives year-round, thanks to a vibrant cultural and commercial life. People come to relax, play sports, shop, and eat well. The attraction is such that on some weekends, over 20,000 visitors arrive. Hotels are fully booked, and the streets are packed. To me, it was the perfect place for an ambitious commercial project.

But first, I had to find the right location. And this is where vision made all the difference.

At the very entrance to the village, right along Highway 15, there was a strategic piece of land. Thousands of cars passed by every day, but few saw its potential. Most saw just a generic access point, a place to drive through. I saw a showcase—a location with unique visibility, accessible from both north and south, a natural stop for tourists just before entering the heart of the village.

My partner from the Faubourg Saint-Sauveur project already owned a Dunkin' Donuts franchise and a carpet store on that site. Between the two buildings was a 70,000-square-foot plot waiting. Across the street, a large 435,000-square-foot vacant lot, difficult to build on due to its clay soil, completed the landscape. Richard, my partner, wanted to make the site profitable. I suggested, Why not build factory outlets, like those in the U.S.?

We contacted the owner of a similar center in Bromont. In exchange for 20% of our company's shares, he would bring his expertise and his connections with major brands. He would also receive a 10% commission on all leases of two years or more.

As with my previous projects, I turned to my designer friend. He proposed a bold sketch: a 28,000-square-foot building on two levels, with an elevator. The ground floor covered 18,000 square feet, and the upper floor 10,000, with an outdoor gallery along its length.

Dealing with the City of Saint-Sauveur wasn't easy. The newly merged municipality had rigid regulations. The city planner refused our permit, claiming our tower was too tall. On advice from an urban planner in Laval, we simply renamed the tower a "belfry"—and everything became compliant. Three months later, the permit was granted.

We also wanted to install glass garage doors instead of windows to allow direct openings to the outside, but the city refused. To compensate, we integrated interior fire doors to ensure smooth flow between units.

We requested three turnkey proposals covering the building, electricity, plumbing, finishing, sidewalks, and paving. The partnership agreement distributed the shares as follows: 40% for me, 40% for Richard, and 20% for our new partner. My co-owner of the land was to receive a fixed amount at the project's end.

This project took two years. Many want to be paid quickly. But to build something like this, one must be willing to wait, to take risks, and to sign personal guarantees. One must believe in the vision. As they say, when the train comes by, you have to get on.

During this time, I thought a lot about the man I had become—less attached to appearances, more rooted in my lifestyle. I lived in an exceptional environment. I was grateful for the challenges, for the failures turned into lessons. I now work six to seven months a year, guided by passion.

The official opening of the Saint-Sauveur Factory Outlets took place in September 1992. It was an immediate success. In this tourist zone, the center remained open even on Sundays, attracting a steady stream of customers.

During a motorhome trip to Palm Springs, California, I had an original idea while visiting celebrity homes. Back in Saint-Sauveur, I spent weeks mapping out the residences of local personalities. I created a tourist circuit, starting at the Faubourg and ending at the Factory Outlets. The flyer titled Visit the Homes of Saint-Sauveur's Celebrities, with photos and addresses, was printed in 25,000 copies.

It was so successful that calls poured in. But soon, celebrities contacted me, furious to see strangers on their properties. Some tourists even settled in with chairs, hoping to spot a star. Facing the threat of lawsuits, I withdrew the brochure and offered my apologies. Quebec is not California.

Traffic remained steady for several years. But by 1997–1998, attendance started to decline. We had anticipated this slowdown. Unlike the often-massive U.S. outlets, our space was limited. Expansion was necessary.

We considered buying the lot across the street, 300,000 square feet, despite a $1.2 million mortgage. A developer wanted to build a St-Hubert restaurant there. The city refused because of the planned sign visible from the highway. Eventually, the restaurant was built in Piedmont.

Chapter 16: Believing in the Vision: A Zoning Battle in Saint-Sauveur

Surrounded by serious and competent people and supported by a vast network of contacts from my time in politics, I was ready to face new challenges. This chapter tells of one of my most defining battles: a political showdown over a single word—zoning.

To discourage us from expanding the factory outlets and to protect existing commercial centers, the municipal administration changed the zoning of the lands we were eyeing, reserving them for recreational uses: cinemas, restaurants, and bars. But I had not said my last word.

The landowner was facing financial difficulties. In 1994, we negotiated the acquisition of the first lot at a modest price. Shortly after, he went bankrupt, and the large parcel slipped from our hands once again. To revive the initiative, we created the limited partnership company Place du Cinema, which became the owner of the small lot. Our designer drew up ambitious plans integrating both parcels into a modern concept: a 12-screen cinema surrounded by restaurants. The idea appealed to the city. Two well-known chains, Nickel and Steak Frites, quickly expressed interest.

Cineplex Odeon collaborated with me for two years to bring the project to life. But at the last moment, pressure from the Sainte-Adèle cinema caused the deal to fall through. Cineplex withdrew. Several tenants left Factory Outlets 1 at the end of their lease. We each had to cover monthly mortgage payments of $5,000. Retail is never tranquil: euphoric during growth, painful when revenues fall short.

I wanted to sell the Faubourg, but my partner refused. Five years of doubts, obstacles, and frustration. Still, I held firm. I persevered. I clung to my vision. Every refusal, every setback was not an end, but a step. I still believed in our project.

We submitted a conditional offer to the bank trust that owned the land, contingent on a zoning change. We renamed the project Factory Outlets 2, and our designer prepared a new plan adapted to the imposed use. Inspired by the outlet villages I had visited in Florida, California, Vermont, and Maine, I wanted to build a unique concept in Quebec.

In 1997, the tide turned: the mayor resigned, replaced by a former classmate from Collège Laval who was more open to our vision. After ten months of discussions, he approved the zoning change. When no one sees the gold, it means there's gold, I kept telling myself.

But the hurdles persisted. The urban planner issued a favorable opinion with conditions. The municipal council voted five to two to send it to public consultation. The day before the assembly, the mayor resigned. A conservative friend, close to the councilors, offered his help in appreciation for my support during the Progressive Conservative leadership race.

That night, the room was packed. Three hundred citizens attended. Opposition was strong, and a petition with 120 signatures was filed. When my turn came, I took the microphone. I became the politician and the salesman again. I presented our plans with passion, reminding everyone that we were two local entrepreneurs, not a multinational, and that our project aimed to energize Saint-Sauveur.

The council ultimately adopted the commercial zoning bylaw.

The bank trust went bankrupt. The Trust General of Canada took over the land. We submitted a new, lower offer. It was accepted.

But my partnership was weakening. My associate refused to take any initiative and left everything on my shoulders. A breakfast meeting marked our split. Richard proposed a deal: he would keep the Faubourg, and I would take Factory Outlets 2, while we remained partners in Factory Outlets 1. I accepted without hesitation. I traded an existing business for a project yet to be built. But I had faith.

On a trip to Prince Edward Island, I had seen houses painted in different colors. I discussed this with my architect, who accepted my idea to have buildings of various colors. I had a knack for selling my ideas to the professionals who worked with me. It was important that they embraced my vision, and sometimes, I embraced their solutions in return.

I contacted Giorgio, then convinced McDonald's to set up in Saint-Sauveur. Bourassa, on his end, wanted to build a 10,000-square-foot fruit store. This project, located on my land, stirred strong opposition in the municipal council. With the former mayor back in the spotlight, we negotiated fair treatment: all shopping centers had to follow the same rule— build on 20% of the land. To ease tensions with the other shopping centers, I agreed to build only on 15% of my project. I sold Bourassa a lot under the same conditions as McDonald's.

Bourassa opened. So did McDonald's and Vidéo Zone. Then I targeted major brands—Reebok and Nike.

The vice president of Nike told me about their Oregon headquarters. I offered him a trip to Mont-Tremblant, where he had skied in his youth. He accepted. During his visit in June 1999, a representative tried to promote a site in Hudson. I discreetly diverted her, spending the day alone with him. He was charmed by Saint-Sauveur and Bourassa's gourmet store, with its giant cold room where customers entered in coats. Captivated, he decided to open a 12,000-square-foot Nike store, visible from the highway.

The delivery deadline was tight but non-negotiable: December.

Following that, Reebok expressed interest in 4,000 square feet. But Nike demanded exclusivity at Factory Outlets 2. So I proposed that Reebok set up in Factory Outlets 1. The investment was significant, but that move triggered a virtuous cycle: Factory Outlets 1 filled up again. Profitability returned.

That was exactly the desired effect.

When everything seems against you, remember this: it's not the majority that defines the truth, but the deep conviction within you. In times of uncertainty, stay the course. The greatest successes are often born in the midst of storms. Faith in your vision and your ability to mobilize, to persuade, and to negotiate—these make all the difference between giving up…and succeeding.

Chapter 17: Therapy

I hesitated for a long time before writing about this subject. Out of modesty, maybe pride. But if this book is to serve a purpose, I must tell everything—even the moments of fragility.

Several years of tension had worn me down. I constantly oscillated between exhilaration and anxiety. What I had lived through in politics—the buried anger, the constant pressure to do everything and succeed alone—had slowly but surely emptied me from the inside. I was exhausted, inwardly broken.

Seeing me deteriorate, a close friend advised me to consult a doctor in Saint-Sauveur. The diagnosis was clear: early-stage depression. He offered two paths—medication or psychotherapy. Without much hope, I chose the latter. I wanted to understand what was wrong. I wanted to heal, not hide.

I couldn't believe it. Me, the tough-skinned, self-assured go-getter, at the end of my rope? It was a shock. But also, somehow, a relief. Finally, someone had put a name to what I had been feeling for far too long.

At the very first session, I unloaded a bag full of memories. My childhood, my relationship with my parents, the dynamic with my sisters, it was like opening a box I had kept locked for too long. I was moved, unsettled. But I was no longer alone.

Twice a week, on Tuesdays and Thursdays after lunch, I went to my appointments. Always at the same time. Always with that knot in my stomach. This therapy lasted two years.

Strangely, this period coincided with the construction of Nike and the Factory Outlets. On the outside, I was the entrepreneur, the leader, and the builder. On the inside, I was living a storm. What a duality. I went from sitting across from a silent psychologist to being on a construction site filled with noise, demands, and decisions. Two worlds. Two faces.

What helped me hold on?

First, simply speaking. Saying what had never been said. Putting words to the pain. Drawing it out, making it visible. Then, the listening. That silent, kind, nonjudgmental listening allowed me to hear myself. Sometimes, there were long silences. And in those silences, I discovered myself.

I also started to write. A journal. Nothing ambitious, just a few lines to try to understand what I was feeling. I poured my fears, anger, doubts, and sometimes, a ray of light into it. Keeping that journal was like drawing a map of my inner world.

Most importantly, I learned one essential thing: I didn't have to carry everything alone. For too long, I had believed that asking for help was a weakness. In reality, it is an immense act of courage. The hardest part wasn't speaking. It was not running away. There were sessions when I wanted to quit. To tell myself this wasn't for me. That I was too strong for this. But no. I held on because I had a goal: to rebuild myself. For others, but mostly for myself.

Oddly enough, as the weeks passed, I began to look forward to those meetings. They had become a need, almost a refuge. I opened up completely, without masks, without strategies. In the last six months, the sessions doubled in length. We went deeper. My psychologist knew the end was near. She helped me understand my deep wounds: Why I felt the need to prove myself so much, why a no always felt like rejection, and why ambition, for me, was also a form of revenge.

I still remember those days when, right after a session, eyes still red, I would arrive at the construction site and resume the role of leader. I sometimes cried at night, silently, unable to stop. But little by little, I learned to accept that vulnerability. To see it not as an enemy, but as an ally.

Ending therapy was one of the hardest decisions. It felt like a mourning. My psychologist framed it this way: "Learning to part is learning to trust what comes next." She was right.

What did I learn most of all?

That healing never happens alone. That external success means nothing if you're empty inside. That real courage sometimes means stopping, listening, and tending to what no longer bleeds but still hurts.

The anger disappeared. It gave way to something more precious: peace.

Today, I can say it with serenity: therapy saved me. I found confidence again. I learned to let go. To free myself from my invisible chains. And most of all, I understood that true power doesn't lie in what we build outside...but in what we repair within.

As Buddha said, "Happiness does not come from acquiring, but from letting go."

Sometimes, it takes more courage to open one door than to walk through a thousand. Acknowledging our flaws and daring to confront them—that's the start of a path toward a new strength. We don't have to wait to hit rock bottom to ask for help. Healing often begins with a single word: "I need help." And in that vulnerability, there is no shame.

The story of the Saint-Sauveur Factory Outlets was not over.

Chapter 18: The Completion of Factory 2

The construction of the Nike store, a 12,000-square-foot building, took six months. Once the foundations and flooring were poured, I immediately began the exterior landscaping. On December 15, the store opened its doors, meeting the company's required date to the letter. It was a first victory in a series of colossal challenges.

After five years of negotiations, Tommy Hilfiger finally agreed to establish itself in Factory Outlets 2. An 8,000-square-foot space was custom-built for this prestigious brand. Shortly thereafter, Rockport joined us as well, with a 4,000-square-foot boutique.

But behind these visible successes was a constant struggle to secure project financing. Traditional banks turned their backs on me. Even the president of the National Bank, where I had been a client for 25 years, refused me a loan. And yet, I had a solid track record: profitable businesses, personal funds available, and no unpaid debts. But in their eyes, I was an overexposed entrepreneur—a man who had borrowed too much. I found myself at the mercy of private lenders.

Then a friend recommended I approach the Caisse Populaire in Saint-Sauveur. Two women in charge of loans welcomed me. I laid out my financial statements, explained my plan, and described my history and the results I had achieved despite adversity. They listened without interrupting, then scheduled a second meeting two weeks later.

A Turning Point

That day remains etched in my memory. The Caisse agreed to finance the work, provided I transferred all my accounts—personal and business—to them. In return, they guaranteed the cancellation of all banking fees. I accepted without hesitation. I had finally found partners who believed in my vision.

Thanks to their support, I was able to bring in new brands like Guess and Cadbury. However, the clay soil intended for the Guess store held a surprise. One morning, the contractor told me we had to remove 29 feet of soil to pour the foundation—a potential financial abyss! I took a deep breath and proposed an alternative solution: remove only eight feet and fill the rest with compacted stones. He agreed. Experience had taught me that in real estate, every problem hides an opportunity for those who look closely.

The situation had reversed: no more hunting for tenants. The Factory Outlets were now attracting the most sought-after retailers. I could afford the luxury of turning down some applications. After seven years of discussions, Black & Decker signed. I built three new buildings: two 12,000-square-foot and one 4,000-square-foot. Only a 2,000-square-foot parcel remained, which I reserved for Polo Ralph Lauren—a brand I had been pursuing since 1992.

A Persistent Vision

For Polo, I envisioned a unique building inspired by small Quebec chapels, complete with a bell tower. When I learned that a church was being demolished in Saint-Antoine, near Saint-Jérôme, I negotiated the purchase of the bell tower for $5,000, pending municipal approval. Proudly, I presented the project to the mayor of Saint-Sauveur, but his response was curt:

"There will always be only one church in Saint-Sauveur."

Rejected. But I wasn't one to get discouraged. In place of a bell tower, I installed four large clocks, each 10 feet in diameter, on the building's facades. The effect was striking. Visible from afar, the store became an iconic landmark.

Eventually, I managed to speak with the president of Jones New York, the new owner of Polo Ralph Lauren. He laughed and said,

"I've never seen a guy so tenacious."

I sent him a full brochure of my achievements, photos of the buildings, and the clock-themed project plans. Impressed, he sent his vice president to Saint-Sauveur, who ultimately approved the Polo Ralph Lauren store.

It was a tremendous victory.

A Major Success

I had borrowed millions, paid tens of thousands in interest and capital annually, but I now owned 75% of a commercial complex of nearly 90,000 square feet. I had built a true high-end outlet village in Quebec, as efficient as those in the U.S., and the project had created several hundred jobs.

Nike, Tommy Hilfiger, Guess, Cadbury, Rockport, Black & Decker, Bourassa… all moved millions in merchandise each year. The center attracted crowds from everywhere. It was a total success—both economically and humanly.

The Saint-Sauveur Factory Outlets In 2002

It was my greatest business accomplishment before turning 70. And every time I return to Saint-Sauveur, my eyes rest on the Factory Outlets with quiet pride. Even though I no longer own them, they remain the fruit of my vision, my courage, and my perseverance.

Chapter 19: Safari

A trip to Tanzania is more than just a safari. It's a journey through the ages, a dive into the origins of humanity, and a continuous wonder in front of untouched, wild nature. It was also, for me, the encounter with a captivating, resilient people and a remarkable woman: Rania.

After watching the IMAX film on the migration of buffalo and wild zebras between Kenya and Tanzania, I felt an irresistible urge to follow their path. Going on a safari was a dream I had always cherished, and this film gave me the motivation I needed to make it happen.

From London, we flew for about twelve hours to Nairobi. On our first evening, we dined at a renowned restaurant, The Carnivore, recommended by our travel agent. Upon entering, we were immediately struck by the enormous charcoal grills cooking meats of gazelle, zebra, crocodile, goose, snake, and many others. We were led to a table marked by a small flag. Meat service continued until we were full—at which point the flag was laid flat on the table. Ah, the zebra! What tender and delicate meat. I was savoring Africa—it was a delight.

The next day, at 10 a.m., we headed for Tanzania. We arrived around 4 p.m. and boarded a Land Rover Jeep, driven by our guide. This vehicle had a roof made of iron bars, giving us an open view of the savannah. Two hours later, exhausted, we entered the first park of our itinerary. No time for a long break—the photo safari began immediately.

Our first encounter was with a leopard near a tree, to the great surprise of our guide, who had only seen two in five years. Our fatigue disappeared instantly. We continued toward a herd of elephants. The male, massive, stood beside our jeep. I filmed the impressive moment. I expected us to continue driving, but we had to wait until the male left the area, as he could become aggressive. On the way back to the lodge, we saw monkeys and three giraffes. Our room looked exactly like what the movies had shown us. Dinner was exquisite, and sleep, restorative.

In the morning, around 7 a.m., we finally discovered the landscape surrounding us. We were in the heart of a multicolored, fragrant floral paradise. A pool built on a cliff overlooked the jungle below. A large terrace hosted a sumptuous buffet, surrounded by abundant flowers and fruit trees. The second safari could finally begin. We witnessed a parade of lions, hundreds of gazelles, wild buffaloes, and zebras. What a show! We felt like children, eyes wide with wonder, scanning every direction.

In Tanzania, in the heart of Africa, we met members of the Hadzabe tribe, the last nomadic people on the continent. We were truly at the edge of the world. After lunch, we headed to a second lodge. Along the way, we paid a local chief in U.S. dollars and visited an African tribe. The inhabitants lived in mud huts with a central stone hearth. The beds were made of branches, covered with animal skins. Barefoot and lightly dressed, the natives seemed to enjoy their way of life despite their poverty.

Kenya Safari

Guards escorted us to our room in the lodge—a typical place deep in the jungle, unfenced. Inside was warm and welcoming, with a large four-sided fireplace, a dining room extending to a terrace, bird fountains, flowering bushes, and a pool. From there, the animals we observed felt almost familiar.

During the next five safaris, we admired countless wild animals. These encounters were made possible thanks to guides who communicated with each other to report sightings. The jeeps rushed toward animal gatherings before they changed direction. The vehicles kicked up so much dust that we were covered in it, so much so that the water from the shower drain ran brown.

One morning, as we passed a group of giraffes, one was lying on the ground. The guide explained that although they are usually seen standing, giraffes do rest in this position sometimes. We witnessed gazelles fleeing from two tigers. We saw thousands of buffalo migrating in synchrony with hundreds of zebras. Sometimes we stopped to let them pass and to admire, among this multitude of animals, the grace of the gazelles, their tiny tails spinning like helicopter blades.

On the morning of our last day there, we left the lodge at 4 a.m. Two hours later, we found a hot air balloon ready to take us on an aerial adventure. Eight passengers boarded to observe the region for over two hours at sunrise. The highlight of the trip was witnessing the migration of thousands of buffalo leaving Kenya for Tanzania.

Suddenly, a lion jumped at a buffalo's throat, bringing it down. The lion let go, but the buffalo stood up, and the fight resumed. Eventually, the lion killed it. Seen from the air, the spectacle was even more impressive. The English pilot managed to land the balloon on a truck moving at the same speed, and we stepped directly onto the vehicle.

We then walked to where the buffalo crossed the river into Tanzania. Violent scenes unfolded under the eyes of crocodiles waiting to devour the carcasses. The smell was nauseating, the scene revolting. However, a breakfast table had been set apart, with a white tablecloth, fresh, fragrant flowers, and porcelain plates. Champagne was poured over strawberries. We enjoyed a breakfast of fruit, eggs, bacon, toast, and coffee. Isolated from the rest of the world, we were surrounded by thousands of flies.

After breakfast, we met the guide who would accompany us for the last days of our journey.

Our next destination was a crater, which we observed from a glass-walled lodge built on the edge of a cliff. The crater lay 2,000 feet below, and the descent took a good half hour.

The next day, we followed steep paths into this world reserved for animals. Thousands of flamingos on a lake made the water appear pink. A little further on, a herd of rhinoceroses wandered slowly. We had lunch there before entering the flower-filled crater, where monkeys, lions, elephants, tigers, giraffes, and colorful birds mingled. The day was magical. We then spent two days at the final lodge, located in a park surrounded by animals.

The Safari: Raw Beauty and Sacred Silence

A safari brings enforced humility. You're no longer the center of the world—you become an observer, a mere guest.

This trip reminded me that material comfort is nothing without inner peace. In Tanzania, I saw people with few possessions but immense smiles. Children playing with a worn-out tire, mothers carrying babies and heavy loads without complaint, and men building with whatever they found.

Africa doesn't give itself easily—it must be earned. It demands slowing down, observing, and feeling. It grabs you by the gut. It's not just a trip; it's a reset.

I found a lesson there: greatness isn't measured by wealth or trophies, but by the ability to love life—even after exile, even after pain.

After three days in an elegant hotel by the sea, we left Africa and returned to London for the final three days of our journey. Pure bliss.

Chapter 20: Purchase Offer

At the beginning of October 2002, I received a purchase offer for the two factory outlets. Without hesitation, I refused it. I had no intention of selling. I still believed I could take them further. But I promised to think it over nonetheless.

The truth was, I was facing a serious financing issue. Banks refused to grant mortgage loans of more than ten years. I had requested twenty-five to balance the payments, but even the credit union said no. This forced me to repay a large amount of capital each month, drastically reducing my profitability. My project was becoming harder to sustain, and I felt the pressure mounting.

A week later, without consulting anyone, I decided to go all in. I made a counteroffer at double the proposed price.

— I won't negotiate downward, I stated, confident in my move.

The fish bit. I was invited to their offices on the 36th floor of Place Ville-Marie. I then had to head to Sherbrooke for a meeting with my travel companions, as we were soon flying to China.

I was greeted by a well-dressed, 68-year-old man with undeniable poise. He led me to a conference room where his son and the real estate agent were waiting. He spoke in English, telling me he owned numerous buildings, but none in Quebec. His portfolio covered Florida, California, Vermont, Vancouver, and Winnipeg. He congratulated me on the success of the factory outlets, which he had visited twice.

Then, with disarming calm, he said:

— Despite all the respect I have for you, sir, it's no.

I didn't flinch.

— I maintain that the whole thing is worth it because it's unique in Quebec.

He looked me straight in the eye.

— I accept your price, but only if we sign immediately.

— OK. I'll be back in an hour. Prepare the contract. Might as well strike while the iron is hot.

I went down to grab a bite to eat. An hour later, the offer was ready. The buyer, who was paying in cash, demanded one hundred days to analyze the transaction and the leases. I signed. And at that exact moment, I felt something strange. The day before, I had nothing to sell. And now, I had just concluded the biggest transaction of my life — as if it were just a detail. My mind was already elsewhere: China.

I left with the original copies. My partners had seven days to sign. It was 2:30 p.m. By 4:00 p.m., I was in Sherbrooke for the travel planning meeting. But I had trouble focusing. I kept thinking about what I had just done.

One of my partners, who held 20% of Factory Outlets 1, was thrilled. He would receive a generous share of the proceeds. But my other two partners reacted very differently. They reproached me for acting alone.

They were right. I had wanted to lead the meeting without interference, without hesitation. I intended to inform them at the right time if things got serious. And they had gotten serious very quickly. The moment dictated its own pace. Could I really be blamed for having made them wealthier?

The partner who owned 25% of Factory Outlets 2 eventually signed, reluctantly. That left my main partner, with whom I co-owned Factory Outlets 1. He had never had to manage them, but now that it was time to sell, he was clinging to this jewel.

He took two days to think it over. Then he signed.

I handed all the documents to the notary's son and the accountants. Shortly after, I guided an engineer and a contractor appointed by the buyer through both sites. Then I turned the page, my heart still a little heavy.

I was about to leave for an eighteen-day trip to China. The sale was underway. An era was ending. But deep down, I knew: I'm not an administrator. What drives me are ideas, projects, and challenges — not the daily management of an empire. I no longer wanted to accumulate, but to live differently. This decision opened the path to something.

Chapter 21: China

I boarded the plane with a strange feeling. Just a few days earlier, I had signed the most important real estate transaction of my life. But now, between two time zones, at 35,000 feet, something else was stirring within me: a deep detachment. We arrived in Beijing after more than 25 hours of travel. The group was made up of about twenty elderly people. Along with a couple of our age, we were the youngest. We would spend most of our time with them.

Upon landing in China, the cultural shock, the excitement, and the discoveries swept me away… but a part of me was elsewhere. I had often dreamed of this trip. Yet this time, something had changed. It was no longer a reward, but a transition.

I wasn't there to relax, but to close a chapter. The group I traveled with was friendly, and the organization was impeccable. But I remained in the background, like a spectator. I smiled, I participated, but deep down, I was reflecting. I realized I had reached a crossroads. I no longer wanted to go back. No more meetings with bankers. No more rent collection. No more pressure to lease the last space or justify maintenance expenses. My energy had always been focused on creation, the initial spark, not on administration, follow-ups, or small worries.

I had sold because I understood that holding onto such an ambitious project alone meant too many risks, too many expectations, too much stability. It was not what I was looking for in this new phase of my life.

Meals were included in our package, but, not drawn to traditional Chinese cuisine, I was always seeking restaurants offering Western food. I even sometimes ate in the Western-style restaurants of the luxury hotels we stayed at.

Arriving in Beijing means finding oneself at the beating heart of China. As the political and cultural capital for centuries, the city embodies both the grandeur of the past empire and the modern country's feverish ambition. Everything here seems designed to impress, to remind the world that China is a millennia-old civilization determined to remain central to the future.

From the first hours, the Forbidden City took my breath away. Behind its high red walls lies a world frozen in time, a labyrinth of palaces and courtyards once ruled by the Ming and Qing emperors. Walking on the worn stones of the throne courtyard makes you feel tiny under the overwhelming authority of the past. Every detail—from the imperial yellow tiles to the carved dragons—speaks of extreme refinement, but also of unyielding discipline.

Not far from there, Tian'anmen Square confronted me with more recent, more troubled history. Immense and austere, it is nonetheless filled with conflicting emotions. Between Mao's Mausoleum and the impassive gaze of the guards, I felt the weight of silence. It is a place both glorified and feared, where history weighs heavily.

But Beijing is not only about the past. It's also a city resolutely turned toward the future. Glass skyscrapers, trendy Sanlitun neighborhoods, and wide avenues filled with hurried, connected crowds… everything moves fast, everything is organized. Yet, down a hidden alley, you stumble upon an old hutong, a traditional neighborhood with low houses where locals still share tea, mahjong games, and daily gossip. Another Beijing survives there: slower, more human.

From the ancient capital to the depths of a vanishing river valley, each step drew me closer to understanding what I was leaving behind.

Our trip to China included an unforgettable six-day cruise on the legendary Yangtze River, the third-longest river in the world. This journey, both majestic and poignant, plunged us into the heart of a transforming China. The scenery was breathtaking. Steep mountain peaks emerged from the mist like in an ancient painting, while the river meandered through the legendary Three Gorges—Qutang, Wu, and Xilinx—true natural cathedrals. In some places, the Yangtze became so narrow that our ship seemed to graze the cliffs, over a thousand feet high.

But behind this raw beauty lay a much darker reality. We were sailing on a path soon to disappear. Just three days after our passage, the locks of the colossal Three Gorges Dam— the largest hydroelectric project ever built—were closed. The flooding of the region began. We stopped in several towns destined to be submerged. Everywhere, the same scene: deserted neighborhoods, gutted homes, empty streets. Everything seemed frozen, awaiting a cataclysm.

The numbers are staggering: 1.8 million people were displaced, sometimes to cities hundreds of kilometers away. Fifteen cities and 116 villages, covering 436 square kilometers, were wiped from the map. The projected cost of $24.5 billion was far exceeded, but for the Chinese government, it was the price of progress—to control flooding, power the country, and ease river transport.

Near the dam, our ship had to be lightened to pass through the last navigable stretch. We disembarked and continued by bus through a lunar landscape. Then, back on the boat, we discovered the dam's titanic structure: a wall of concrete over 400 feet high, stretching endlessly. At the top, we were fascinated by the giant lifts that allowed boats to pass through different water levels, like elevators for giants.

This Yangtze journey wasn't just a tourist cruise. It felt like pausing between two eras, between natural splendor, engineering feats, and human tragedy. We were witnessing the end of a thousand-year-old world, swallowed in the name of the future.

After the cruise, we visited the Great Wall of China, one of the seven wonders of the world, said to be visible from the Moon. Yet I wasn't impressed by what seemed like just a small pathway flanked by stone walls a few feet high. Only its length was striking, with no visible beginning or end— just a narrow road stretching as far as the eye could see.

We spent a day in Xi'an, the most visited city in China, where, in 1974, a farmer discovered an army of terracotta soldiers buried underground. This discovery dates back to Emperor Qin Shi Huang, who had these life-sized statues built to protect his tomb. Upon his death, he was buried with the soldiers, horses, and chariots of clay. To preserve the secret, all workers involved were buried alive.

Our trip ended in Shanghai, where we spent three days. We left the group to explore the city at our own pace. If New York is immense, Shanghai is even more so, with its modern and imposing towers. One morning, we took the subway, where no one spoke English. We used two maps—one in English and one in Chinese—comparing landmarks to find our way. We took a cruise on the Huangpu River, which splits Shanghai into two. We also visited a 96-story hotel, the tallest in the world, with rooms arranged in a circular arc. From the top, the reception desk looked like a tiny point far below.

Shanghai struck me as a waking dream, a futuristic vision rising on the banks of the Huangpu. Unlike Beijing, rooted in imperial tradition, Shanghai embodies modernity, openness, and a certain Westernized boldness. It's a city of all contrasts, all rhythms—a city that never sleeps.

But Shanghai is not just science fiction. It's also a living memory. Walking along the Bund, the emblematic riverside promenade, I discovered an older Shanghai—the one of foreign concessions, colonial banks, and art deco hotels. This district gave me the strange feeling of walking through a period film, between remnants of a bygone world and the gaze of a conquering China.

I also took time to get lost in the old town. In Yuyuan, the traditional gardens offered a moment of calm: wooden pavilions, lotus-edged ponds, zigzag bridges. In the heart of a megacity, this place breathes slowness, Taoist wisdom, and the beauty of silence. It's here I understood that Shanghai doesn't reject its past—it embraces it, even elevates it amid its modern rush.

At nightfall, neon lights flicker on, illuminated boats glide along the river, and the entire city becomes a spectacle. I dined in a small restaurant in the Xintiandi district, where old lilongs have been restored to host galleries, cafés, and terraces. It was both lively and intimate—a perfect metaphor for Shanghai itself: a vast city that still knows how to speak gently to those who listen.

What's most striking in China is its population of over 1.3 billion. Cleanliness is exemplary, and nature is a national priority. Trees abound, parks and waterways are numerous, well-lit, and lined with trails. The Chinese people are respectful, very polite, and always ready to help. We truly enjoyed our trip.

When I returned to Quebec, I knew something had shifted. I no longer wanted to accumulate. I wanted to transmit, simplify, and lighten. China had been the backdrop to one of my greatest inner transformations. And in the silence of the return flight, high above the Pacific, I made myself a promise:

The next adventure won't be real estate. It will be human.

Chapter 22: Final Sale

Naturally, my return was marked by a multitude of questions. One hundred days had passed between the signing of the offer and the final sale. The days were long, not only for me, but also for the tenants and the few service companies at the Factory Outlets who, being well-informed about the negotiations, were worried about their future.

Around mid-January, the buyer began to show some concern. His demands suddenly increased, and I felt he was trying to make me bend—perhaps one last attempt before closing the deal. The question that seemed to haunt him was, was the deal really worth all that money?

I had no intention of giving in. I reinforced my notary— who had been handling the file alone so far—by bringing in my lawyer as a teammate. A week before the sale was to be finalized, the buyer played his last card by inviting me to lunch alone with his wife, an industrial psychologist. I knew very well that this lunch was just a pretext to probe me, to dissect me. But, exhausting my last reserves of patience, I answered all their questions during the hour they spent analyzing me, feigning ignorance and calm.

D-Day—the final signing—arrived on Friday, January 31, 2003. I went to the office at 9 a.m., accompanied by my notary and my lawyer. The buyer seemed unsettled by my lawyer's presence. He tried to steer the discussion toward three contentious points, but these issues were resolved within half an hour, thanks to my lawyer's efficiency. Having completed his mission, my lawyer withdrew, leaving the rest of the day ahead.

The rest of the day was devoted to reviewing the documents stacked on the table. On one side, my notary and me; on the other, the father and son, the real estate agent, another notary, and an accountant. The tension was palpable, but the gears of the sale were turning. Shortly before 4 p.m., the sale of the Factory Outlets was finally concluded.

Why sell? The buyer had obtained a loan covering 90% of the purchase price, with a 25-year repayment term. As we were leaving, he introduced me to the representative of the National Bank, the one who had financed the deal. A quiet rage rose in me at that moment. As I shook his hand, I said with a forced smile:

—It's ironic. You refused me a loan, claiming my project wasn't profitable.

At that moment, everything became clear. Access to financing for a young company like mine had been an uphill battle. I had managed to get loans, but only for short durations—10 years at most. This meant high monthly payments, constant pressure, and an obligation for immediate profitability. In contrast, my buyer had obtained a 25-year loan, drastically reducing his payments and allowing him far more flexibility in his investment.

That was the injustice of the system. Large companies or well-established buyers had access to favorable financial terms, while entrepreneurs like me were suffocated by the weight of repayments. Even though I was managing a viable project, the lack of banking support had put me in a corner.

I understood: in this world, it's not always skills or vision that make the difference, but access to capital and time. Small players, strangled by unsuitable financing, are often forced to sell. That day, I accepted this hard truth. And I sold.

On Monday, February 3, 2003, I went for the first time in my life to collect checks of such magnitude. At 58 years old, it was the first time I held such an enormous sum in my hands. Twelve years after successfully completing a commercial project that had significantly increased tourist traffic to Saint-Sauveur, the outcome was finally there.

My buyer, with a satisfied look, compared the factory outlets to a rose garden he had picked at just the right moment. I let him say it with a slight smile.

PART THREE
The Retirement I Dreamed Of

For as long as I can remember, I have had one dream: never to get bored in retirement. I wanted to stay busy, to keep creating, and above all, to travel all over the world. After about fifteen years in politics, and following my resignation, I took two years of semi-retirement. Two years to reflect, to realize that I no longer wanted to work nonstop, but to find a way to be self-employed, succeed at one project at a time, and take breaks between them to savor life.

I spent 17 years in development, creating projects. When I sold the Factories, financially comfortable, I dreamed of turning my retirement into a playground: to have a stimulating occupation but also to enjoy my freedom to the fullest and travel to the four corners of the world.

The next chapter, Chance and I, says that anything is possible. Turn the page and…

Chapter 23: Private Lending: Risky Financial Autonomy and Helping Others

At 59, while I was doing renovations on my home in Sainte-Adèle, an idea came to me. My contractor, who was redoing my roof, told me about his restaurant and his need for financing. After being turned down by the bank because of his mortgage, he didn't know where to turn. Seeing an investment opportunity, I offered him a $20,000 loan at 8% interest as a first mortgage. He accepted. That was my first private loan—but certainly not my last.

That experience was a revelation. My past at Household Finance, where I managed loans and collections, along with my real estate training, had prepared me without me even realizing it. From then on, private lending became much more than just an investment: it allowed me to have full control over my finances while helping people.

Helping… and earning a living honestly.

There was a time in my life when I chose to help differently. For twenty years, I offered private first-mortgage loans to people society seemed to have abandoned. It wasn't about money—it was about humanity.

Here's a truth I never hid: during those twenty years of private lending, I earned money. Yes, people paid interest. It was a service—and like any service, it had a cost.

But what I did was neither exploitative nor speculative. It was humane financing, with a clear logic: their situation didn't allow for traditional bank loans, but that didn't mean they didn't deserve anything. Quite the contrary.

I helped people who had gone through storms—bankruptcy, divorce, loss, or other setbacks—find their footing again. I didn't lend to perfect profiles. I lent to imperfect but brave people. And in return, I received fair interest, proportional to the risk I took.

It was neither charity nor greed. It was an exchange. A contract. A balance between solidarity and responsibility.

And often, beyond repayment, what I received was worth far more: a thank you, a relieved look, a saved home, a life back on track. That's when I truly realized what I had built—for them and for myself.

I never saw myself as a banker or investor. I was a bridge, a relay between the fall and the restart. Every loan was, for me, an act of trust. I didn't lend to their past—I lent to their desire to bounce back.

I always worked transparently, surrounded by notaries, with clear conditions. But most importantly, with heart. I didn't want to imprison— I wanted to liberate. And I saw stories come back to life. Homes saved. Lives restructured. People regaining their dignity, step by step.

This chapter of my life marked me deeply. It showed me there are a thousand ways to help. I simply reached out where others withdrew.

The Story of Marc and Suzanne

I remember them as if it were yesterday. A couple in their forties, two children, a modest suburban home. They had everything to be happy… until Marc lost his job and then fell ill. The debts piled up, credit cards maxed out, and one day, they were on the brink of losing their home.

The banks turned their backs: bad credit, unstable income, too risky. But I welcomed them—calmly, without judgment. We talked at length. It wasn't just a case file—it was a family fighting to keep their roof.

I offered them a first mortgage loan. The interest was clear—not abusive, but enough to cover my risk and earn a living. Everything was done before a notary, with full transparency.

Thanks to that loan, they paid off their arrears, avoided foreclosure, and could breathe again. Three years later, Marc found a stable job. They repaid the loan in full. On the day of the final payment, they came to see me with big smiles.

Suzanne told me, You were the only one who believed in us. You did more than lend money—you gave us back our dignity.

That day, I knew that this profession—done with heart and honesty—could truly change lives.

For twenty years, I managed about forty mortgage loans, exclusively in first mortgage positions. My principle was simple: borrowers paid interest only, and the capital was recovered at loan maturity. While I did have to repossess a few homes and lost some interest, I never lost capital.

The advantage of private lending is that it allows financing for people rejected by the traditional banking system: entrepreneurs, self-employed workers, business owners, or those who have gone through bankruptcy, divorce, or loss. Rather than betting on their solvency, I secured my loans on the value of their property. This way, I offered them a quick solution while securing my investment.

I was well-supported: a secretary, a notary, a lawyer, an accountant, and a handyman—carpenter, plumber, electrician. When a house needed to be repossessed, I supervised its renovation and resold it at a profit, covering my expenses and consolidating my capital.

To succeed, I relied on:

— A precise evaluation of the property and real estate market

— The ability to make quick decisions to seize opportunities

— A reliable professional network to secure every transaction

— Respect for financial commitments, ensuring my reputation and borrower loyalty

— A clientele built through word-of-mouth, from banks and satisfied former clients

My biggest loan was quite an adventure. I met a client who wanted to borrow a certain amount for six months to complete the construction of his house before obtaining a bank loan. I accepted at a rate of 12% annually. He only wanted six months, so he offered me 15% for that period, which I accepted. After nine months, he repaid me in full.

Nearly two years later, he contacted me again for a meeting in Mirabel. He needed a large loan for a construction project. After more than ten years of private lending, at age 69, I began to consider full retirement.

Out of curiosity, I went to his office near Saint-Jérôme, right on the edge of Highway 15. His project was in a flood zone and included three 6,000-square-foot foundations, plus a 10,000-square-foot foundation with 12-foot-high Styrofoam block walls filled with concrete, but no roof or floor.

The site included a 5,000-square-foot office with living space, unfinished outside, on a 145,000-square-foot lot. A real construction site—but in an exceptional location. He had all the city permits from Mirabel and Quebec environmental approvals. His project was ambitious: a specialized center for homebuilders with spaces for kitchens, bathrooms, lighting, plumbing, and construction materials. All his plans, drafted by an architect, were approved by the city.

He wanted a seven-figure loan at 12% interest to repay his debts and continue the project. In exchange, I would hold the first mortgage on the land and existing buildings. I asked for a week to think.

If I accepted, it would be my biggest loan—and a major risk. But the location was incredible: right along Highway 15, northbound, near exit 39. No matter where you came from, access was ideal.

Having dealt with him before and having been repaid without issue, I decided to go into the project with a partner who agreed to invest with me. We finalized a two-year loan.

The Problems Begin

The first year went well: he made his monthly payments on time. But then trouble began—he couldn't find tenants. I kept telling him to find solutions, to change his plans, as the project was too expensive. I didn't want to take it over—at 70, I didn't want the responsibility. He tried to sell it but failed. Finally, he considered bankruptcy.

After discussion, we agreed he would hand over the project in exchange for canceling the mortgage. I now owned a project with no clear future.

Chapter 24: My Last Loan At 70

I tried to sell it, but every buyer backed out: too risky, flood zone, no water or sewer lines. His office had only a well and a septic system for the bathroom.

During a meeting with the city, I learned that municipal services were located along Route 158, over two kilometers from the site. Connecting would be too expensive. In the fall, I left for Florida for six months, leaving the plans in his office, which he now rented.

The Mini-Storage Idea

During the winter, I thought of a solution. I've always believed every problem has an answer. In Florida, I noticed the popularity of mini-storage units. Why not turn this project into a mini-storage complex?

I visited several facilities and researched how they operated, their costs, and their profitability. The bigger the project, the more profitable it becomes. Back in Quebec, I met with my architect to draft plans and a site layout. He told me I could build about 400 mini-storage units ranging from 50 to 400 square feet on that land—but I'd need sprinklers in each unit.

I contacted Dépotium, a Quebec leader based in Toronto. After touring their sites, I wasn't impressed with their model, and they considered my project unprofitable. However, they confirmed that the Laurentians had strong potential for storage and recommended installing heated floors.

The Challenge Begins

Everyone around me was skeptical: the land was too expensive; profitability would take years. The project would cost millions, not including the land and the $75,000 needed to demolish the existing concrete structure. But those objections only fueled me more. You have to believe in yourself and your ideas.

I studied the plans for months and decided to keep the 10,000-square-foot building and turn it into a two-story complex. On the ground floor, I added 20×50-foot garages on all four sides. Upstairs, I created over 50 fireproof units from 20 to 50 square feet, accessible by freight elevator.

Mini-Storage 15 Nord

The three existing foundations of 60×100 feet were used. Outside, we built 10×20-foot garages, and inside, 10-foot corridors with 5×20-foot units.

For three summers, from May to November, we built the project by self-financing. I recruited a strong team, and we bought all materials ourselves. The floors were heated, and the concrete block walls were 9 feet high, making the units extremely secure. With no water or sewer lines, we couldn't install sprinklers. To compensate, all ceilings and doors were fire-resistant metal, and the exterior was clad in red and black corrugated metal. After the first phase, I identified unused space for parking. I got permits for two buildings of 60×100 feet and 60×80 feet, and we continued construction.

In the second year, we finally opened, and rentals quickly reached capacity. The location was ideal; the units were made of concrete and had heated floors. We built over 400 units, ranging from 20 to 400 square feet.

We succeeded.

Mini-Storage 15 Nord in Mirabel, along Highway 15, was born. In the fall of 2018, at age 73 and with no successor, we sold it, financing a portion of the sale price over five years.

Risk, perseverance, passion, and work: those are the keys to success.

A Life Lesson

At 70, I thought I had long been retired. But this last loan reminded me that one is never safe from a challenge. It was demanding, sometimes exhausting, but it was also a victory.

I knew that private loans, even though they can help and save families, always carry great risks. The secret is to have the courage and strength to face them, to turn failure into a solution.

This project was my last great battle in the business world. After it, I was finally able to turn the page and dedicate myself to what I had always dreamed of: traveling, undertaking differently, and enjoying life.

Another Lesson

Looking back, I realize that private lending was much more than a profession. It was my way of helping, my way of reconciling money with humanity.

I saw families reborn, homes preserved, dreams revived. I also learned that taking a risk is not only a matter of money, but of faith: faith in others, faith in their ability to rise again.

For over twenty years, we moved forward this way, balancing prudence and boldness, numbers and beating hearts. Those years of private lending allowed us to live freely, work at our own pace, and above all, travel the world with the peace of mind that comes from doing good.

If I had to sum up this period in one sentence, it would be this:

"Private lending taught me that helping sometimes means accepting risk. But when that risk is guided by the heart, it can transform lives — and grant you the freedom to fully live your own."

Chapter 25: Freedom

Retirement does not fall from the sky. It is not something you endure, but something you choose and prepare for. Just as one chooses to have a child at 23 or at 30, retirement depends on the moment when one feels ready, on the efforts made beforehand, and on the vision one has of it.

Throughout my life, I worked, invested, took risks, faced trials, and rose to challenges. It was not only about succeeding in the moment: it was also about giving myself, one day, the freedom to live the retirement I had always dreamed of. This choice was not imposed by age or by rules, but by an inner decision: I wanted to be free.

At 60, I chose freedom. Not an escape, nor a whim, but a response to an inner calling that had been gently knocking at my door for years: to leave. To see the world.

These stories are not mere travel anecdotes. They are chapters of life, living proof that a dream has no expiration date. Each destination was first a discreet desire, buried beneath obligations, and later transformed into a shining reality.

At this age, one no longer travels to impress. One travels to feel alive, to celebrate the life one has built, and to honor the time that remains.

Traveling as a Second Life

"One might think it was money that allowed me to live these adventures. But no: it was not money that carried me, it was desire. True wealth lies in the courage to dare and the strength to turn a dream into reality."

In the chapters that follow, I will take you through mountain roads and burning deserts, into the heart of ancient cities, and along the shores of vast seas. You will ride with me on trains crossing endless landscapes, walk through alleys heavy with centuries of history, and see, through my eyes, how vast… and beautiful the Earth can be.

These journeys are far more than postcards. They are my second life. After years of politics, projects, and battles, I needed a space that belonged entirely to me. Traveling was my retirement— not a rest, but a rebirth.

Freedom Regained

I say it with conviction: traveling, for me, was tasting freedom.

- The freedom to drive without a schedule.

- The freedom to choose the back road instead of the highway.

- The freedom to breathe without agenda or pressure, after decades where every day was dictated by obligations and decisions.

Traveling was relearning how to listen to the wind, to smell the fragrance of a marketplace, to sit on a foreign bench simply to watch life go by.

Travel as a Mirror

Each destination was a mirror.

- Scotland, with its wild roads and mysterious lochs, reminded me that I could still take on new challenges.

- Tunisia, with its sandstorms and infinite desert, taught me that freedom always comes with a share of risk.

- Jordan, with the majesty of Petra, showed me that some dreams, even old ones, deserve to be pursued to the very end.

Thus, each journey became a life lesson. Not merely landscapes, but intimate experiences that helped me better understand the world… and better understand myself.

These journeys are my freedom written in black and white. My testimony is that even at 60, one can begin a new life. They are not simple stories, but proof:

- That it is never too late to learn, even to ride a motorcycle when you once thought you hated it.

- That it is never too late to dream, even if society tells you it's time to slow down.

- That it is never too late to feel young, even when the calendar says otherwise.

An Invitation

What follows is not an inventory of countries visited. It is a hymn to freedom.

I share these memories to pass on a simple message:

👉 Every sincere desire deserves to be pursued.

👉 Every life deserves moments of daring.

👉 And it is never too late to dream, to desire, to achieve.

So, ready your curiosity. Turn the page. Climb behind me, helmet fastened tight. And let's set off together, toward the unknown—where every road becomes a promise and every horizon a victory.

Chapter 26: Motorcycle

Take motorcycles, for example—they used to be nothing but a nuisance to me. I had spent most of my life complaining about them and even forbade my sons from owning one. Yet, since my youth, I have had both a car and motorcycle license.

One day, as I watched some bikers parked in Saint-Sauveur, the idea hit me: what if I tried it too? I had no more challenges ahead of me, and at 60, it was time to leave my comfort zone. I signed up for a driving course in Saint-Jérôme—four evenings of training, two in a parking lot and two on the road with a small motorcycle. On the last night, riding under pouring rain, I still wasn't convinced I liked motorcycles.

A friend advised me to meet the owner of Honda Saint-Hyacinthe. During our meeting, I explained I had never owned a motorcycle and didn't know which model to choose, but I wanted a comfortable one. He showed me a Gold Wing, had me sit on it, and said,

— You're tall enough; your feet touch the ground.

He had me convinced.

I decided to buy a used 2000 Honda Gold Wing—a beautiful machine, pale green, fully equipped, and with low mileage. My condition: someone had to help me train before I hit the road. The following Friday, I picked it up. After two hours of practice, they deemed me ready.

So, on Friday, May 14, 2004, during rush hour, I hit the road alone, heading toward Saint-Jérôme. Two hours later, exhausted from the nervous tension, I stopped for a well-earned break. Around 8 p.m., after a good meal, I rode back to Sainte-Adèle, thrilled by the calm road. The passion was starting to take root.

Motorcycling in Scotland: The Birth of a Passion

I dreamed of a big motorcycle trip—and that dream came true. A contractor friend who had built several buildings at the Factory Outlets told me he was leaving in two weeks for a 10-day motorcycle trip to Scotland with two friends. He explained that the adventure included eight days of riding BMWs, each person covering their own expenses. One of their friends already in Scotland handled the route, hotel bookings, restaurants, and motorcycle rentals.

— No problem, reserve a big one for me! I told him without hesitation.

The excitement was palpable. As soon as we arrived in Scotland, we picked up our bikes, and I took twenty minutes to get used to mine before we set off. Each day, we rode about 450 km on stunning roads, winding through lush valleys, majestic mountains, and mysterious lochs. The wind kissed my face as we cruised through the Highlands, alongside crystal-clear rivers and through charming villages where time seemed to stand still.

We stopped in Edinburgh, the capital, and enjoyed breakfast in a quaint restaurant, admiring the medieval architecture and cobblestone alleys steeped in history. Later, we passed by spectacular green golf courses—true landscape gems reflecting Scotland's passion for the sport. At times, the road hugged the North Atlantic coast, revealing wild beaches and windswept cliffs where sheep roamed freely.

The landscapes changed constantly, offering breathtaking views at every turn. Scottish roads are a biker's paradise: well-maintained, low traffic, and full of elevation changes and stunning vistas. Some passes led us to remote plateaus overlooking golden-lit valleys. In the evenings, we gathered in cozy pubs, savoring traditional dishes like haggis with fine Scotch whisky. Bills were always split five ways, reinforcing the camaraderie of the trip.

The atmosphere was lively, filled with laughter, stories, and the joy of shared experiences on the road.

Scotland, October 2005

That trip was a revelation. After 25 years of RV travel, I discovered a new way to explore the world: by motorcycle. All my senses were heightened—the rush of wind, the scent of forests and moors, the engine's roar beneath my hands. It was absolute freedom, a mode of travel where you become one with the road.

As always, I loved diving fully into each experience. And this journey was just the beginning of a long motorcycling adventure. Soon after, a friend told me about a French company that specialized in Harley-Davidson Road trips across various countries.

Curious, I contacted them and learned their next expedition was in Tunisia—15 days riding through deserts and oases on motorcycles. Motivated by this new adventure, I bought a second used bike—a Harley.

This trip to Scotland had awakened a new desire in me: for the open road, endless horizons, and an engine humming beneath the stars.

On The Road of Mirages in Tunisia

The Grand Run is a Harley-Davidson raid with full support. It is organized by a licensed professional, HOG France, and sponsored by Harley dealerships. Road captains and safety marshals lead or follow the group, accompanied by a surgeon.

At 6 p.m., every rider had only one wish: to start their engine. Suddenly, Jean-Marc, the "general" (road captain), gave the command: "Start engines!" The convoy rolled out. I understood why they called him that—disciplined and firm, he led with an iron grip. At 58, this former textile industrialist had sold everything six years earlier to dedicate himself to organizing such rides in Morocco, Libya, Syria, Jordan, and Turkey.

Besides the bikes, a support car, two trucks—one for luggage and one for fuel—and a mechanical assistance vehicle with two spare bikes made up the caravan. A couple from Spain, four Belgians, and nine Canadians joined the French. From Lyon to Bourg-lès-Valence, cold rain followed us for over 100 km.

The next morning, we left at 6:30 a.m. It was a short night. Light rain, freezing cold, and dark riding until 8 a.m. After 225 km, we reached the Marseille port and boarded the ferry to Tunis.

Arrival in Tunisia

We arrived late morning at the port of La Goulette, Tunis. After customs, we were escorted by the Tunisian National Guard to Sidi Bou Saïd, a beautiful blue-and-white village overlooking the Gulf of Tunis. Then on to Gammarth, a high-society resort area, where we stayed at the Abou Nawas Hotel. A dip in the pool and sea before drinks and dinner rounded off our first Tunisian day.

We had over 400 km to cover. The weather was beautiful. We headed toward Kairouan, a sacred city of history and religion. It is the first holy city of the Maghreb and the fourth most sacred in the world after Mecca. After lunch, we visited the Roman ruins of Sbeitla, a vast ancient city with an arch, a grand temple, and many columns still standing. As clouds gathered, our general gave the signal to depart. Everyone donned rain gear. At 4 p.m., a downpour hit hard.

The temperature dropped suddenly. It was dark, cold, and the wind howled through our coats. Hail battered our faces. Then a sandstorm struck. Visibility vanished. Our bikes leaned dangerously. We struggled to keep the balance. Safety protocols went out the window. We focused only on the road, scattered with shrubs like in a Western. It took 2.5 hours to travel 110 km to Gafsa, where we stayed at the Jugurtha Palace Hotel.

What an adventure! And to think—we paid for this! Now I understand why they called it a raid.

Toward the South and the Desert

We left for Métlaoui under a sunny sky. With our clean bikes, we headed south toward the mountain oases. We visited Medes, an old village perched above deep gorges—an extraordinary view! Red, ochre, and pink desert mountains stretched before us. Suddenly, a palm grove emerged in the middle of the desert. We reached the Algerian border and had lunch at the Tamerlan Palace Hotel, built in the middle of nowhere.

Then on winding roads to Chebika oasis, one of Tunisia's most beautiful. We arrived in Tozeur, at the Sahara's edge, and crossed its grand palm grove before reaching Nafta, the "Princess of the Desert." In this season, dates were harvested and featured in every meal. After over 300 km, we settled at the Sahara Palace Hotel.

The next day, we crossed the Chott El Jerid, a sea of sand and salt. This 100 km straight road was surreal. Depending on the sun's angle, one sees shimmering mirages—water, sky, sand, and salt blending.

We continued to Douz, a magnificent oasis where desert nomads and oasis dwellers meet. After 200 km, we arrived at the Mehari Hotel. In the afternoon, we rode quads, and at sunset, we mounted camels for a slow desert ride ending with cocktails among the dunes. Unforgettable!

Back North

We visited Matamata, known for its troglodyte homes dug by Berbers centuries ago—like a sci-fi movie set. It was used in Star Wars. We continued through Kasar Hallouf, Kasar Hadada, and the Kours loop, passing Chenini and Kasar Ouled Soltan. After 350 km, we arrived in Tataouine and stayed at the Sangho Privileges Hotel, built in traditional Berber style.

Heading north, we passed through Médenine and Gabès, where we enjoyed a beach lunch under tents. In El Diem, we saw the largest Roman amphitheater in Tunisia (closed due to Ramadan). We drove through olive groves to Mahdia and stayed in a luxurious five-star hotel.

The raid was ending. We returned to Tunis via a scenic coastal road usually closed to tourists but opened just for us. Back in La Goulette, we waited to board the ferry. Some were already talking about the next trip. A friend whispered:

You must visit Petra in Jordan before you die!

Which I did... on a motorcycle, of course.

And so ended our Tunisian adventure: 2,600 km traveled, flawless organization, constant support, and strict safety, with over 2,000 Tunisian police mobilized for our convoy.

Chapter 27: On The Trail Of Lawrence Of Arabia

In 2006, the desert called us once again. After China, after the roads of Asia, a new adventure was taking shape: Syria, Jordan, and Egypt. Three names, three mythical lands, three childhood dreams that were about to become reality. And always the same companion, the motorcycle, like a thread linking eras and civilizations.

Syria and Damascus

Syria came first, with Damascus, a city scented with spices, its markets echoing with ancient voices. There, I discovered a people of disarming generosity. One memory in particular remains etched in me: at the entrance of a school, children rushed toward us, their arms full of roses, which they offered as treasures. Their smiles, their innocence, contrasted with the image of a country often depicted as closed. That day, I understood that travel is not measured only in kilometers, but in suspended moments.

Jordan and Petra

Then came Jordan, and Petra, the rose-red city nestled in the heart of the mountains. We arrived at dawn, when the sun's rays strike the rock-hewn façades and set them ablaze.

To reach this mythical site, I had to mount a donkey. Fear clenched my stomach with each step; the cliffs seemed ready to swallow me whole. But the beauty that unfolded was worth the price: the Treasury, majestic, rose before me like an apparition. It was one of the most intense moments of my life as a traveler.

In the Footsteps of the Pharaohs, in Egypt,

This was our last journey with the general and the French group, and perhaps the most striking. Egypt welcomed us with its contrasts: the eternity of its monuments and the fragility of life.

We began with a five-day river cruise on the Nile. The valley, flanked by arid deserts, teemed with life. The peasants of the Nile lived much as their ancestors had a thousand years ago. While most visitors come for the monuments, what remains etched in our memory is the life of its people, their timeless way of being, almost outside of time itself.

My Egyptian journey began on the Mediterranean shores of Alexandria, where history mingles with the sea breeze. The roar of my engine echoed along the Corniche as I left the city, behind me the Qaitbay Fortress and the modern library, heir to the legendary ancient one.

Then, fate struck. Right before me, a Frenchman, accompanied by his wife, took a curve too wide. I saw him soar through the air and fall into a ravine some thirty feet deep. The entire convoy stopped. The doctor traveling with us rushed down, and I decided to follow him. The man was still breathing, but his face was badly injured. The doctor asked me to speak to him while he tended to his wife. No one else descended. Finally, he shouted to the general: "Send men down!"

Two ambulances eventually arrived and took them to the hospital. Another group retrieved the motorcycle. The general, implacable, gave a brief order: "Engines!"

And we left. That decision chilled many of us, yet it seemed the only possible outcome, as some riders already refused to continue. At the hotel, we received the terrible news: the man had died of a pancreatic hemorrhage. His wife rushed back to France, survived after a major operation. That is what a motorcycle raid is: the unexpected, the risk, and sometimes the cruel price of the road.

Some claimed we were riding too fast. But at the end of the trip, we learned that the Frenchman had been sick, with the flu, and was taking medication. He had likely dozed off at the handlebars of his motorcycle...

We resumed our journey with heavy hearts. The roar of engines once again echoed along the Corniche, but now each acceleration carried the weight of tragedy. The road to Cairo became an odyssey through desert and endless plains. The hot wind whipped my face as we crossed villages where time seemed frozen: palm groves, white-domed mosques, bustling markets, donkey-drawn carts. Each kilometer was a dive into authentic Egypt.

Arriving in Cairo, the contrast was overwhelming. The chaotic traffic became an exhilarating challenge: cars, tuk-tuks, pedestrians… The motorcycle slipped through like a fish in a torrent. But beyond the turmoil, it was history that seized us.

The Pyramids of Giza appeared on the horizon, imposing, defying the centuries. I parked my motorcycle facing those stone giants and approached the Sphinx, its enigmatic gaze fixed on eternity.

We traveled 1,600 km in 13 days across Egypt.

On camelback, I crossed golden dunes, gazing at the majestic silhouette of the pyramids under the setting sun. Then, in the heart of Cairo, the Khan El Khalili bazaar engulfed us. The scents of spices, the gleam of copper lamps, and the lively alleys carried us into another world. Between a cup of mint tea and the stories of merchants, I understood that Egypt was not just an open-air museum: it was a land of encounters, emotions, and contradictions.

Throughout the journey, our thoughts never strayed from our two French companions, victims of the terrible accident. Their absence loomed like a shadow over our adventures, a reminder that life, like the road, can change in an instant.

Our Egyptian journey ended before the Pyramids of Giza. Never would I have imagined seeing forty motorcycles lined up at the foot of those millennia-old wonders. The contrast between the noisy modernity of our machines and the silent majesty of those monuments will forever remain engraved in my memory.

We traveled 1,600 km in 13 days across Egypt.

Chapter 28: CORCICA South Africa, And Peru

Before shipping our bikes back to Quebec, we explored Corsica, Sardinia, and Sicily.

The ferry from Marseille brought us to Ajaccio. The Mediterranean air, scented with eucalyptus and pine, welcomed us with open arms.

We traveled along Corsica's coast to Pino. Every turn revealed cliffs, sea views, and unforgettable sunsets. We stayed in inns or small B&Bs. Locals were warm and hospitable, often clearing their garages for our bikes. We enjoyed Corsican cuisine and wines. After 10 days, we reached Bonifacio, a cliff-top citadel. Then came Port Torres in Sardinia, followed by Palermo in Sicily.

In Sicily, we explored near Mount Etna and stayed in Cefalù. From Palermo, a ferry took us to Naples. In pouring rain, we rode to Nice—892 kilometers later. Customs told us our bikes had to return home after two years abroad. Shipping them back ended a remarkable journey.

South Africa

In April 2010, we rode 2,700 kilometers across South Africa on a 13-day tour. From the vineyards in Stellenbosch to the dry terrain of the Little Karoo, each day brought new scenery. We passed hot springs, caves, and ostrich farms.

The Great Karoo felt like another planet. On Route R355, the longest gravel road in the country, we admired surreal landscapes. The Garden Route offered stunning coastlines, and in Tsitsikamma Park, we crossed the Storms River suspension bridge.

We saw the amphitheater of the Drakensberg Mountains and Tugela Falls. The Sani Pass ascent revealed Lesotho's remote heights. At Coffee Bay, we marveled at the 'Hole in the Wall.' We ended at Cape Agulhas, where the Indian and Atlantic Oceans meet. Ten days on Harley-Davidsons—unforgettable.

Peru

We landed in Lima and picked up trail bikes. A flat tire marked the start of our trip to Paracas. There, we visited the Ballestas Islands—Peru's mini-Galápagos—teeming with sea lions, penguins, and seabirds. Next came Nazca, where we glimpsed the mysterious ancient geoglyphs. At Puno on Lake Titicaca, we visited floating reed islands. In Pisac, altitude posed a challenge, but our mechanic adjusted the carbs to help us climb.

The highlight was Machu Picchu. At over 2,400 meters above sea level, the Incan city stunned us. Its mystical energy and perfectly aligned terraces made it unforgettable. Traveling in Peru required physical endurance, but with friends from Abitibi, it became a rewarding adventure.

Chapter 29: Western Canada and The U.S.

I enjoy driving through the La Vérendrye Wildlife Reserve on Route 117—it's a peaceful, pleasant road that always puts me at ease. On this trip, we were heading to Rouyn to visit friends we had once traveled to Peru with.

Route 117 becomes Highway 66 in Ontario, and in Kirkland Lake, we turned onto Highway 11. It's the northernmost route across Ontario, running east to west through the province. A few mining towns near Quebec and a succession of small villages. I was very surprised to see that all the signs were first in French, then in English—even government signs. Many signs displayed very Québécois names like Villeneuve, Veilleux, Poulain, Gauvin, Boisvert, etc. In Hearst, we learned that 95% of people speak French and have both primary and secondary schools in their language. The town is nicknamed "Little Quebec." It's also the national capital of moose!

Thunder Bay, Ontario, a city of 110,000 people, sits near the American border in the northwest of Lake Superior. The day began with a light drizzle, followed by a fine rain that stayed with us for several hours. The long, narrow, and straight road that runs through a dense and endless forest was mind-numbingly dull. Suddenly, two massive moose burst out of the woods right in front of us. They crossed the road with slow, majestic steps, giving our bikes a disdainful glance. For 200 kilometers, they were the only living beings we saw... oh yes, and a magnificent pheasant in autumnal colors.

Then, from Long Lac to Thunder Bay, another 300 kilometers through the woods, this time sprinkled with tiny villages bearing Indigenous names. Near Beardmore, we passed Lake

Reflection, aptly named, with the water mirroring the cliffs above it. Landscapes like these make us feel small in the face of such majestic nature! The most stunning views are between Red Rock and Thunder Bay, where the road overlooks Lake Superior.

Moose Jaw, Saskatchewan, Wakamow Heights B&B. In the evening, we spent a few hours at the Temple Gardens Mineral Spa Resort, which was a much-needed relief after all those days on the motorcycle.

The next day, we visited the Chinese tunnels. Dug under the city's streets, the Moose Jaw tunnels have both a tragic and fascinating history. They reveal the harsh living conditions of hundreds of Chinese workers who helped build the Canadian railway to earn their "ticket to fortune." A few decades later (in the 1920s), during Prohibition, Al Capone is said to have come to Moose Jaw to oversee his smuggling operations; the city's tunnels provided a perfect network to evade the police.

Lake Louise, Fairmont: we spent the night in this luxurious hotel.

From Hope, British Columbia, where we stayed at Evergreen B&B. The owner told us that Sylvester Stallone had shot his first film there, Rambo: First Blood. In the evening, he lent us the movie, and the next day, we crossed the same bridge Stallone used in the film. We also admired the cliff he climbs while being attacked by a helicopter. Hope is a beautiful village.

Upon arriving in Vancouver, we visited several iconic places: Gastown, Chinatown, Stanley Park, and the Capilano Suspension Bridge. We then took the ferry to Victoria and explored the magnificent Brentwood Gardens on Vancouver Island. To end the day, we toured Victoria on a three-wheeled bicycle pedaled by a student.

We then took the ferry from Sidney to Anacortes, Washington, and then followed Route 20, recommended by the Ride Atlas. The route was splendid: we crossed the Cascades National Park and admired the turquoise color of the river and Ross Lake, reminiscent of Lake Louise. At the end of the day, we walked the wooden sidewalks of the western-style village of Winthrop—a true movie set experience. On the road, we spotted a deer crossing right in front of us.

The next morning, we took our time before leaving, as the temperature was close to 0°C. Heading toward Coulee Dam, we paused to pick apples in an orchard. Then we followed Routes 174 and 2 to Spokane, before crossing Idaho, nicknamed the "potato kingdom," though we didn't see any potato fields. We quickly reached Montana, where Highway 90 was a pleasant ride, winding through the mountains. The air was icy.

We continued to Jackson, Wyoming, where we stayed at the Ranch Inn. This authentically western town is filled with typical Wild West shops and draws many tourists and artists. Having arrived early, we enjoyed strolling through its picturesque streets.

Our journey then led us through Yellowstone Park. We were fascinated by the wildlife along the road and the erupting geysers, especially Old Faithful—impressive in both power and consistency. Unable to find accommodation within the park, we continued to Elephant Head Lodge, lost in the middle of nowhere.

The next morning, we took Route 14 to leave the region—an exit just as difficult as the entry. After a stop in Cody to visit the Buffalo Bill Museum, which highlights the history of the Wild West and Indigenous peoples, we headed to Buffalo. The road, lined with spectacular landscapes, was home to herds of wild horses and cattle.

We then continued to Deadwood, a town rich in history, especially that of Bill Hickok. Today, Deadwood is also a popular destination for gambling enthusiasts, with many small casinos open all night. After a long stop to service our motorcycles at Harley in Gillette, we reached Custer, where we admired the Crazy Horse Mountain. This colossal monument, still under construction, will be ten times larger than Mount Rushmore, our next stop. We were awestruck by the monumental sculptures of Washington, Jefferson, Roosevelt, and Lincoln.

Our journey then took us to Sturgis, the mecca for motorcyclists. Every year, the town hosts the largest motorcycle rally in the world. The atmosphere was electric.

A true pilgrimage for two-wheel enthusiasts.

We took Route 34, covering 230 kilometers of nearly deserted landscapes with no services or gas stations—just a few isolated farms and many herds of cattle. Back on Highway 90, we were battered by violent gusts of wind. This journey plunged us into the heart of mythical America, with endless roads, western towns, and breathtaking landscapes. An unforgettable experience, forever etched in our memories.

Chapter 30: Oceania Continent

Adventure in Australia and New Zealand

My father had a business partner in the extermination field whom I met when I was 17. He was from Australia and never stopped talking about his homeland, describing it as the most beautiful country in the world. I promised myself I would visit it one day.

We began our adventure in Perth, the most isolated city on the planet from its neighbors. Unfortunately, we didn't have time to fully enjoy it—just a one-night stop at Miss Maud Hotel before boarding the famous Indian Pacific Train. What I remember most about Perth is its world-renowned surfing beaches, the blue waters of the Indian Ocean, and the scorching heat—already 38°C by 9 a.m.

From the moment we boarded the train, we were confronted with cramped cabins, even though we were in Gold Class. The space was so tight that we constantly had to open and close our suitcases to access our belongings.

After four days and three nights crossing the desert, we were relieved to arrive in Sydney, although the landscape was fascinating, with vast arid plains, ghost mining towns, and occasional sightings of kangaroos and sheep.

We sighed with relief upon arriving in Sydney. This cosmopolitan city, built around one of the most beautiful bays in the world, charmed us with its Opera House, Harbor Bridge, and relaxed atmosphere. A walk along Bondi Beach or through the Royal Botanic Gardens, followed by a drink at the harbor at sunset, was a perfect moment.

After Sydney, we headed to Melbourne, where we enjoyed the cultural buzz and the refined ambiance of this artistic city. A surprise awaited us:

during a walk, two women kindly offered us tickets to the Australian Open. We watched an exciting match between Gaël Monfils and a Brazilian player. The atmosphere was electric, with the crowd erupting at every exchange.

We then followed the spectacular Great Ocean Road, winding and bordered by cliffs plunging into the Southern Ocean. We saw koalas in the eucalyptus trees and admired the famous Twelve Apostles—natural sculptures shaped by wind and waves. A stop in Apollo Bay allowed us to enjoy excellent fish and chips facing the sea.

Our journey continued to Strathalbyn, a picturesque village with Scottish inspiration in the heart of a wine region. It was a restful stop before beginning a new crossing: the Outback.

We crossed the entire cutback aboard a large Toyota 4x4 equipped with a massive steel bumper, almost like a war vehicle. And it wasn't a luxury—on these remote and desert roads of the Australian Outback, accidents with wildlife are frequent, especially at sunrise and sunset. The bumper, as massive as it was, became vital protection.

The cut-back is a long stretch of solitary road, sometimes straight for hundreds of kilometers, where you feel both tiny and free. Few stations, few villages, almost no one in sight for hours. The immense sky, the red hues of the desert, the wind lifting the red dust… The isolation is total, but the raw beauty of the landscape more than makes up for it. It's in this wild part that Australia reveals itself in its most authentic version.

We saw several kangaroos—sometimes hopping in the distance, sometimes sadly crushed on the road. Their number is impressive: they appear without warning, especially at night, and can cause serious accidents. Hence, the need to slow down, stay alert, and have a solid vehicle.

At one point, we stopped on the roadside for a break. There, we were lucky to see a group of sleeping koalas in the eucalyptus trees. These iconic little marsupials are even lazier than one might think—they sometimes sleep more than 20 hours a day, perched in trees, indifferent to everything. Watching them brought a sense of peace. It's easy to understand why Australians see them as symbols of calm and gentleness.

In Coober Pedy, the opal capital of the world, we slept in an underground hotel—a welcome shelter from the extreme heat. We visited a mine, sifted sand for opals, and touched firsthand the tough reality of these gem seekers.

Then, in the Red Center, we witnessed the color changes of the mythical Uluru (Ayers Rock) and the Kata Tjuta mountains, bathed in golden light at sunset. A sacred moment.

After a pause in Alice Springs, we continued to Darwin, with a stop at the fascinating Devils Marbles—huge rocks balanced in the desert. The heat broke records: 48°C under a cloudless sky. Despite that, the sunset over the rocks was magnificent.

In Kakadu National Park, saltwater crocodiles awaited us. During a tour on the Adelaide River, we saw these predators leap out of the water to grab meat held by our guide—a mix of thrill and fascination.

We also viewed the rock paintings of Nourlangie, vivid traces of a millennia-old past.

In Darwin, we left our big Toyota. We flew to Cairns, gateway to the Great Barrier Reef. Unfortunately, jellyfish season made swimming risky. Thanks to full-body suits, we still managed to dive among the corals and multicolored fish. A several-meter-long shark even swam beneath us—an unforgettable thrill.

New Zealand, Land of Extremes and Wonders

Then, a change of scenery: off to New Zealand, the land of the "Kiwis." Upon arrival, we rented Harley-Davidsons to explore this wild land. Here, no snakes, no crocodiles, but landscapes of incredible beauty.

New Zealand is the realm of raw nature, a young, inventive country, resolutely geared toward adventure. From the moment we landed, I felt I had entered another world. Here, mountains seem to rise from the depths of the sea, forests vibrate with ancient energy, and the human-sized cities harmoniously blend into spectacular surroundings.

Queenstown: The Cradle of Adrenaline

Considered the world capital of extreme sports, Queenstown is a gem nestled by Lake Wakatipu, surrounded by snow-capped peaks. It's here that bungee jumping was born, a New Zealand invention made famous by A.J. Hackett. The Kawarau Bridge, where it all began, still challenges the boldest.

Standing on the platform, feet tied, you must overcome your fear and dive into the void... a suspended second of eternity.

But Queenstown doesn't stop there. The boldest can try zorbing, another local invention where you roll down a hill inside a giant transparent plastic ball. Laughter guaranteed—especially when water is added!

Further north, Rotorua is a strange and fascinating city, known for its steam vents, bubbling mud pools, and its distinctive sulfur smell. It's also a major center of Māori culture.

I attended a traditional evening in a reconstructed village, where songs, dances, and legends immersed me in the history of a proud people deeply connected to the land.

Wellington: The Capital of Wind and Creativity

Further south, Wellington charmed me with its artistic energy. Theater, cinema, design—everything seems to pulse with quiet boldness.

It's home to the Weta Workshop studio, which contributed to the Lord of the Rings films shot throughout the country. The interactive and captivating Te Papa Museum gracefully tells the natural and human story of New Zealand.

Auckland: The City of Sails

Auckland, nicknamed the "City of Sails," is the country's largest city. Cosmopolitan, dynamic, and open to the sea, it's surrounded by extinct volcanoes and stunning beaches.

It's the perfect starting point to explore nearby bays, go sailing, or simply enjoy a coffee while watching yachts dance on the water.

In New Zealand, every road is a movie set. From the fjords of Milford Sound to the golden beaches of Abel Tasman, from the volcanoes of Tongariro to the glaciers of the west coast, it feels like crossing several continents in one country.

And everywhere, the sincere kindness of the Kiwis, their deep respect for nature, and their simple joy of life. It's a country that dares to invent, to welcome, to fully live.

We ended our journey in Auckland, the City of Sails. A cruise through the harbor, dotted with green islets and fresh seafood, was a gentle conclusion to this long journey across the Oceania continent.

This trip was a true epic, a series of strong emotions and discoveries. If travel shapes youth, it also challenges old age. But what a joy it was to fulfil this dream from the other side of the world!

Chapter 31: Russia

Saint Petersburg, the Venice of the North

It fully deserves its nickname, "The Venice of the North." A boat ride along the Neva River and its countless canals offers a majestic introduction to this city conceived as an imperial dream. As we glided under ornate bridges, we caught glimpses of the grand silhouettes of Saint Isaac's Cathedral and the Church of the Savior on Spilled Blood— masterpieces that give the city a unique and almost otherworldly aura.

At each bridge we crossed, I couldn't help but admire the lighting poles fixed to the movable sections. The question burned on my lips: how is electricity managed when the bridge pivots to let boats pass? Even our guide didn't know the answer.

We waited. Then, like a perfectly choreographed scene, the bridge began its rotation. The electrical connections detached at the ends with impressive precision, then reconnected just as easily when the bridge closed. A feat of discreet but fascinating engineering.

Visiting the Church of the Savior on Spilled Blood was one of the highlights of the trip. Built on the very site where Tsar Alexander II was assassinated, it embodies the tragic history of Tsarist Russia. Its façade is a bold blend of multi-colored domes, arches, and frescoes, but the interior truly dazzled me—walls covered with incredibly fine mosaics, depicting scenes from the New Testament like living paintings.

The Catherine Palace and Park in Pushkin

While the heart of Saint Petersburg captivated me, it was in the town of Pushkin, about thirty kilometers south, that I felt a more intimate sense of wonder. There lies Catherine Palace, a jewel of Russian baroque architecture, surrounded by the vast Pushkin Park. This estate is a hymn to imperial grandeur and classical elegance.

From the entrance, the palace impresses with its blue and white façade adorned with golden elements. But it is the mythical and mysterious Amber Room that draws all the attention. Reconstructed after disappearing during World War II, it remains a symbol of beauty and human perseverance. You enter almost on tiptoe, as if into a sanctuary.

The park, meanwhile, offers a soothing contrast. Between the tree-lined paths, small bridges, peaceful lakes, and romantic pavilions, I felt a rare sense of peace. Here, nature and lifestyle meet in perfect harmony. It was one of those places where time seems suspended, where every turn invites daydreaming.

Its magnificent parks are listed as UNESCO World Heritage Sites. The park is so vast that it is divided into seven distinct zones.

We visited the Church of the Savior on Spilled Blood, built on the very spot where Tsar Alexander II was assassinated on March 13, 1881. The exterior is a striking combination of shapes and colors, while the interior is a pure marvel. The mosaics tell the story of the New Testament with extraordinary richness and finesse.

We then visited Saint Isaac's Cathedral, one of the largest churches in Saint Petersburg. Inside, an exhibit tells the incredible story of its construction through authentic historical documents, plans, and models.

The Peter and Paul Fortress, birthplace of the city, now houses several museums tracing the foundation and evolution of Saint Petersburg.

After six days of wandering in Saint Petersburg, I found it hard to leave this fascinating city… This stay left a deep impression on me. Before setting foot there, I had a thousand images in my mind…

Moscow

After a transfer to the station, we boarded the Sapan train to Moscow. Upon arrival, our private guide took us on a city tour. Moscow is a fascinating city, a unique blend of architectural masterpieces and cutting-edge modern buildings.

Red Square, with its 73,000 square meters of brickwork, is a must-see experience. We took time to capture this iconic site surrounded by the Kremlin walls, Lenin's Mausoleum, Saint Basil's Cathedral, the Resurrection Gate, the GUM department store, and the State Historical Museum of Russia.

We continued our visit with Saint Basil's Cathedral, the iconic masterpiece of Red Square, built in 1561 by order of Russia's first tsar, Ivan the Terrible, to commemorate the victory over the Khanate of Kazan.

Alexander Park, the oldest public park in Moscow, runs along the Kremlin wall. It is divided into three gardens and contains sculptures, fountains, and mosaics inspired by popular fairy tales. We witnessed the changing of the guard at the Tomb of the Unknown Soldier, an impressive ceremony held every hour in front of the eternal flame.

Our visit continued with the Moscow Metro, a true underground palace, reputed to be one of the most beautiful in the world. It is a vast museum, with stunning interiors, statues, bas-reliefs, and decorative compositions—paintings, mosaics, and stained glass. The metro is impeccably clean, and its escalator is the longest in the world.

We then explored Arbat Street, one of the oldest in Moscow. Once a trade route, it became, in the 18th century, a prominent spot frequented by artists and the Russian intelligentsia.

One of the highlights of the trip was visiting Bunker 42, a real bunker built in the 1950s by order of Stalin as a nuclear shelter for senior USSR officials. Located 65 meters underground, it covers more than 700 square meters.

During the visit, a nuclear alert simulation was triggered: lights out, blaring sirens—a gripping and impressive experience.

Star City

To visit, we had to obtain special authorization from the Russian embassy in Montreal. During our visit, Quebec astronaut David Saint-Jacques was present, preparing for a space mission.

We explored the renowned Russian cosmonaut training center, formerly a closed military town. This site houses fascinating equipment and laboratories, including the world's largest space centrifuge. We learned about astronauts' daily lives in orbit and the many practical details of living in space.

Kazan is home to many cultural and historical sites, including the Kazan Kremlin, declared a World Heritage Site in 2000. This complex is an exceptional testimony to Tatar historical continuity and cultural diversity.

In the afternoon, we visited the Qol Sharif Mosque and the Islamic Culture Center. Then we were transferred to the station to board the night train to Yekaterinburg.

Listvyanka is a small town located 70 kilometers from Irkutsk, near where the Angara River separates from Lake Baikal. Despite its modest size, Listvyanka is one of Siberia's most popular tourist spots. This village, inhabited for 300 years, even hosted a shipbuilding workshop.

During our excursion, we visited Saint Nicholas Church, built in the 19th century. Then we took the funicular to the top of the mountain of the same name, where we discovered a panoramic observation platform offering views of Lake Baikal, the Angara River, and the legendary Shaman Rock Vos.

A cruise on Lake Baikal is a wonderful opportunity to admire the lake's immensity in a short time. We boarded a very comfortable boat from Listvyanka, sailing toward the wild and unspoiled landscapes of the northern lake, passing rocky shores and sandy bays inaccessible by land. A true treasure of eastern Russia!

We had planned to experience the banyan (the Russian sauna). Traditionally, it is a small wooden house, a log cabin with a stove covered with stones used to produce hot steam. For centuries, Russians have believed that the banyan purifies not only the body but also the soul.

Unfortunately, we found the place poorly maintained and decided to skip the experience.

We were supposed to reach Beijing by taking the Trans-Siberian Railway, but we were very disappointed with this mode of transport. In the end, we decided to take a flight to Beijing.

We spent two nights in a luxurious hotel in the city center. We explored the city by day and night.

Chapter 32: Dubai

Several times, people have asked me which motorcycle trips I've enjoyed the most. Among my many adventures, Syria, Jordan, Corsica, and the American West remain unforgettable memories. But if I had to choose one that particularly stood out, it would undoubtedly be Dubai and the United Arab Emirates.

There are must-see destinations for motorcycle enthusiasts around the world, especially in North America and Europe. Yet for adventurers seeking a different and more exotic experience, Dubai offers a unique opportunity. Here, you combine the thrill of riding a Harley-Davidson with the discovery of contrasting landscapes: dizzying skyscrapers, endless desert, rugged mountains, and crystal-clear seas. It was a true change of scenery, but with a touch of familiarity thanks to Serge Brouillet, a Québécois based there, who rented us the bikes and organized our tour through his company, Prestige Moto—a private, tailor-made trip for two people.

Discovering Dubai and its treasures

Before venturing out of the city, we took time to familiarize ourselves with our bikes by exploring Dubai. We rode to the iconic Palm Jumeirah, an artificial archipelago shaped like a palm tree, home to lavish celebrity residences and the famous Atlantis hotel with its spectacular water park. We then visited the Jumeirah Mosque, the sail-shaped Burj Al Arab hotel, and wandered through the Gold and Spice Souks, where the oriental atmosphere was at its peak.

One of the most surprising places in Dubai was the Dubai Miracle Garden—a huge floral park in the middle of the desert, where millions of flowers form breathtaking plant sculptures. The contrast with the surrounding arid environment was striking.

Heading to Abu Dhabi

We left Dubai and drove into the Emirati countryside toward Abu Dhabi, the capital of the richest emirate. There, we admired lavish palaces and visited a heritage village that depicted traditional Bedouin life. The Sheikh Zayed Grand Mosque, dazzlingly white and adorned with marble and gold, amazed us with its majesty.

After these discoveries, we hit the road inland, crossing golden dunes to reach the Liwa Oasis, where we spent the night in a luxurious hotel in the heart of the desert.

On the road to Al Ain

The next day, we resumed our journey to Al Ain, a city known for its cultural heritage and camel market. Crossing the desert offered us spectacular landscapes, with endless dunes and wind-sculpted rock formations. A stop at the Al Jahili Fort, a preserved historical monument, allowed us to better understand the history of the Emirates.

Between mountains and sea: Fujairah

We continued toward Fujairah, taking winding roads through the Jebel Hafeez mountains. This stretch was one of the most memorable of the trip. The switchbacks offered stunning views of lunar-like terrain, and once we passed through the mountains, the sea appeared in all its splendor.

The contrast between the arid landscape and the turquoise waters of the Gulf of Oman was breathtaking. In Fujairah, we visited the oldest mosque in the Emirates and enjoyed a well-deserved swim on a sandy beach.

Ras Al Khaimah and the gates of Oman

Leaving Fujairah, we followed the coast to reach Ras Al Khaimah, a lesser-known emirate full of natural treasures. One of the highlights was a dhow excursion to the Musandam fjord, often called the "Norway of Arabia." This rugged marine landscape, with its steep cliffs and deep blue waters, was enchanting. We were lucky to be escorted by curious dolphins, and we snorkeled to explore the seabed.

Returning to Dubai via the northern emirates

On our return trip, we passed through the emirates of Umm Al-Quwain, Ajman, and Sharjah, discovering amazing contrasts between wealth and simplicity. In Sharjah, the Blue Souk immersed us in a bewitching oriental atmosphere, filled with the scents of spices, traditional carpets, and artisanal objects.

Back in Dubai, we extended our stay by two days to enjoy the city's unique energy a bit longer. It was the perfect time to relax and relive our adventure through a recap video of our journey, carefully created by our agency.

This motorcycle trip through the Emirates was undoubtedly one of the most beautiful and disorienting of my life. Between the dazzling modernity of Dubai, the grandeur of Abu Dhabi, the splendor of the mountains, and the tranquility of the oases, each stage brought its share of surprises and emotions—a perfect blend of adventure, discovery, and pleasure in a setting both luxurious and wild. An experience to relive without hesitation.

Chapter 33: Antarctica, the Realm of Eternal Winter

This trip was one of the most impactful experiences of my life. Departing from Chile, sailing along the Patagonian coast, crossing the dreaded Drake Passage to reach Antarctica, and then heading north to Brazil was an unforgettable adventure. Each stage of this journey offered breathtaking landscapes, fascinating encounters, and moments of pure wonder.

The departure from Chile was filled with excitement. From the port of Valparaíso, our ship set off toward the Chilean fjords, revealing stunning views of glaciers and steep mountains. The cold became more biting as we sailed further south, approaching one of the most remote and inhospitable places on Earth.

The Drake Passage, known for its tumultuous waters, gave us a rough but exhilarating crossing. Then came Antarctica—a world of ice and silence, where nature reigns supreme. Icebergs in surreal shapes, colonies of penguins, and whales surfacing from the depths left an indelible mark on me.

After several days exploring this white desert, we resumed our journey north along the Argentine coast. As we approached Buenos Aires, the capital of Argentina, we were struck by the city's vibrant energy. Tango echoed in the streets, cafés buzzed with lively discussions, and elegant architecture recalled the country's European past. We tasted local delicacies, especially the famous Argentine grills, and immersed ourselves in the unique atmosphere of this captivating metropolis.

Continuing north, we followed the Brazilian coast, where the landscape changed radically. Arriving in Rio de Janeiro, the sight of Sugarloaf Mountain and Christ the Redeemer overlooking the bay left us speechless. The beaches of Copacabana and Ipanema pulsed with festive energy, while samba music filled the air. The contrast between lush nature, the mountains, and the urban bustle made this final stage unforgettable.

Our arrival under blazing sunshine, in stark contrast to the polar cold we had just left behind, marked the end of an extraordinary adventure. This journey was a true lesson in humility and wonder before the grandeur of the world.

There are places on Earth that defy imagination—spaces where man is merely a tolerated visitor in the face of nature's relentless force. Antarctica is one of them. A continent of ice, of absolute purity, where extreme cold reigns supreme and every gust of wind seems to carry the echo of a forgotten world.

From the moment I arrived, I was overwhelmed by the vast expanse of ice stretching before me. Antarctica offers no cities, no roads, no familiar landmarks. It is a white desert, even more hostile than the dunes of the Sahara or the Mongolian plateaus. Here, all is silence—except for the distant cry of seabirds and the deep rumble of icebergs breaking away from the ice shelf.

I walked on a sheet of ice that has covered the ground for millions of years, trapping within its layers the secrets of Earth's climate. Beneath my feet lay remnants of ancient times—air bubbles frozen in ice, witnesses to a distant past when Antarctica, once lush and green, was home to thriving forests.

Today, this continent, the coldest and windiest on the planet, sees temperatures that can drop below -80°C, challenging any form of permanent human life.

Yet life exists here—discreet but resilient. On the horizon, a colony of emperor penguins marched in single file, stoically braving the icy wind. These astonishing creatures, able to survive the harsh

Antarctic winter, embody the strength of adaptation. Nearby, a Weddell seal rested on the ice, indifferent to my presence, while petrels and skuas circled in the sky—black silhouettes against a backdrop of endless white.

Far from being just a frozen desert, Antarctica is also a living record of the explorers who braved its extreme conditions.

I thought of Ernest Shackleton and his legendary 1914 expedition, when his ship, the Endurance, was trapped in ice, leaving his crew to fight heroically for survival. I saw images of Roald Amundsen, the first to reach the South Pole in 1911, narrowly beating the ill-fated Robert Falcon Scott, who perished on the return journey. These men, driven by indomitable courage, carved their names into the legend of this unforgiving continent.

But Antarctica is not only a land of conquest. It is also a unique scientific laboratory, where researchers from around the world study the climate, stars, and life beneath the ice. In these isolated stations, teams investigate global warming, tracking signs of a world in flux.

Here, more than anywhere else, the fragility of our planet is palpable—the accelerated melting of glaciers, the thinning ice shelf, the impact of climate change on ocean currents.

Faced with this immensity, I felt infinitely small. There was a kind of purity in this place that few spots on Earth can offer. Far from the noise of civilization, Antarctica commands humility and respect. It reminds us that we are but fleeting passengers on this planet—visitors who must abide by the laws of a world older and more powerful than ourselves.

As the sun slowly dipped toward the horizon, casting pink hues on the sparkling ice, I felt a deep peace. This was no ordinary landscape, but a natural cathedral where even the silence seemed sacred. The wind blew, the ice sang beneath my feet, and in that suspended moment, I witnessed eternity.

Chapter 34: Carnivals, A Global Spectacle

Brazil – The Rio Carnival And The Amazonian Adventure

I have often been asked what one of the most spectacular things I had seen during my travels was. I have been fortunate to witness incredible landscapes, majestic panoramas, and monuments steeped in history. But among all of these, one memory remains deeply etched within me: the Rio Carnival. It is not just a celebration; it is an explosion of life, a moment when an entire people dance, sing, and rise in a fervor that goes beyond words.

The Amazon, a journey into the heart of life

On January 31, 2016, we left Miami to reach Manaus, the gateway to the Amazon. It was there that our four-day cruise on the mythical river began, in the heart of a still wild, vast, and captivating world.

Sailing on the Amazon, the largest river in the world, meant entering a realm where nature reigns supreme. The banks seemed endless, covered with vegetation so dense it formed an impenetrable green wall. The sounds of the jungle were everywhere: cries of unknown birds, the rustle of monkeys, the discreet hiss of unseen animals. This natural symphony wrapped around us like a primitive music, older than man.

We were lucky enough to observe emblematic animals: sloths swaying slowly from the branches, anacondas slithering through the murky waters, alligators with gleaming eyes emerging at dusk, and above all, those astonishing pink dolphins that leapt out unexpectedly, as if to remind us of the hidden magic of these mysterious waters.

At the village of Paradiso, a memorable stop allowed us to discover a way of life in fragile yet harmonious balance with nature. Children played barefoot in the damp earth, their radiant smiles defying poverty. We even tried our hand at piranha fishing: two catches were enough to remind us that these small creatures carried a fearsome ferocity.

But perhaps it was the canoe ride through the igapós — those flooded forests — that moved me the most. Gliding silently between submerged trunks, under a dim light filtered through the foliage, I felt as if I were traveling outside of time, as if I had crossed a threshold into an original world. Everything was silence and mystery, beauty and fragility. That suspended moment will forever remain engraved in my memory.

The greatest street party in the world

After this interlude at the heart of life, we took a flight from Manaus to Salvador, via Brasília, to dive into a whole other kind of frenzy: the Bahia Carnival.

For six days (and up to twelve with the extended festivities), the city ignites to the rhythm of African-inspired percussion. Imagine 2.5 million people, from all regions of Brazil and around the world, flooding the streets in a riot of sounds, colors, and movement.

The heart of the celebration takes place in Campo Grande, Barra-Ondina, and Pelourinho. There, the "electric trios" — immense trucks equipped with sound systems and musicians — move slowly through the crowd. Everyone dances around them, swept up in a whirlwind of pure energy. We ventured in for a moment, but the density of people and the frenzy were such that we quickly returned to our perch in the cabin, from where we could watch the celebration without fear of being carried away. For four days, we witnessed this popular jubilation, hypnotized by the contagious power of the music.

The Iguaçu Falls: a natural wonder

From Salvador, we flew to Foz do Iguaçu, with a stopover in São Paulo. The falls awaited us, majestic, monumental. Listed as a UNESCO World Heritage site, they stretch for nearly three kilometers, sharing their force between Argentina (80%) and Brazil (20%).

On the Brazilian side, the panorama is breathtaking: dozens of waterfalls tumble down from dizzying heights in a deafening roar. But it was on the Argentine side that we truly touched the soul of this place: winding trails, walkways above the torrents, refreshing mist clinging to the skin. Each step revealed a new perspective, more impressive than the last. In front of the "Garganta del Diablo," the Devil's Throat, we felt both the beauty and the brutality of nature.

Rio de Janeiro: the greatest show on earth

Then came the grand finale: Rio and its carnival.

The heart of this world-famous celebration beats in the Sambadrome, a gigantic avenue-stadium designed by Oscar Niemeyer. Each evening, six samba schools, each with up to 5,000 participants, take turns offering parades of unimaginable creativity. Costumes of feathers and sequins sparkle under the floodlights.

Gigantic floats rival each other in madness and extravagance. The rhythms of samba invade the body — it is impossible to resist.

We entered the Sambadrome at 6 p.m. and did not leave until dawn, at 6 a.m. Twelve hours passed unnoticed, swept away by a human tide carried by a single passion. A jury of about forty judges scrutinizes every detail: the perfection of the percussion, the creativity of the floats, the choreography, the respect for the theme. Everything is evaluated with utmost seriousness, because here the celebration is also a fierce competition.

But what strikes the most is the people's fervor. The Rio Carnival is not just a spectacle; it is a religion of joy, a national communion. In this tumult of sounds, colors, and movements, I felt carried into a waking dream.

NEW ORLEANS – THE CARNIVAL OF SOUL AND JAZZ

Changing continents also means changing carnival. After Brazil, the year before was Louisiana, and more precisely, New Orleans, birthplace of jazz and a stronghold of cultural blending. Here, the carnival does not have the flamboyant excess of Rio, but it has a depth and authenticity that make it just as fascinating.

A carriage ride through the old town plunges us into another time, while a steamboat trip on the Mississippi reminds us of the vibrant history of this majestic river. But it is above all by strolling through the French Quarter that we discovered the true beauty of the place. A mesmerizing blend of Spanish, French, and African traditions permeates every corner, every façade, every shaded square.

The restaurants with spicy aromas, the lively cafés, the bars with electric atmospheres, and the small shops bordering inner courtyards gave us the impression of being elsewhere — almost in Brussels, almost in Quebec — but always with a unique touch: that of the wrought-iron balconies and flowered windows that tell the city's mixed history.

Bourbon Street: the party that never ends

When the sun sets, Bourbon Street awakens. The street bursts into neon lights and interwoven music.

Here, a jazz band makes its brass resonate; there, a rock group whips up the crowd. Bars with wide-open doors overflow with dance and laughter. Colorful beads fly from balconies and land on passersby, transforming each walker into an actor in the spectacle. To my great surprise, I received two without even asking—a sign that the celebration chooses its chosen ones at random.

The street becomes a living theater where amazed tourists, passionate musicians, improvised dancers, and locals faithful to this tradition cross paths, all keeping the heartbeat of their city alive.

It was impossible to leave New Orleans without a stop at the famous Café du Monde. There, under the arcades, we tasted the iconic beignets: square, crispy, drowned under a shower of powdered sugar. A true sweet sin, especially when accompanied by a Hurricane, that powerful rum-based cocktail well worthy of its name.

Here, carnival is a sensory experience: one lives it as much with the ears and eyes as with the palate.

TWO CARNIVALS, TWO SOULS, ONE SAME TRUTH

In Rio as in New Orleans, carnival transcends the everyday. But it does so in two radically different ways.

– Rio is excess, grandeur, a firework of colors and sounds that illuminates the entire world. One feels the force of a whole people rising in collective fervor.

– New Orleans is intimacy, human warmth, the celebration tucked into every alley, every balcony, every note of jazz. Here, carnival tells a story: that of a unique cultural blend, of a city that has transformed its wounds and mixtures into a celebration of life.

Two carnivals, two universes. One flamboyant, the other captivating. But one common truth: everywhere, carnival is a triumph of joy over the everyday.

The Rio Carnival is not just a parade—it's a celebration of joy, peace, and togetherness. The samba schools bring together thousands of people from all social backgrounds, united by a shared passion. This collective fervor, festive spirit, and explosion of color and music make Rio's Carnival a one-of-a-kind event. I can say without hesitation that it is one of the most impressive spectacles I've ever witnessed in my life. A magical moment.

Chapter 35: Paradise and the Victoria Falls

If paradise exists, it is here, on the island of Zanzibar, specifically at the Ras Nungwi Resort. This piece of Tanzanian land, set in the turquoise waters of the Indian Ocean, is far from the image one might have of Tanzania. Long under the rule of the sultans of Oman, Zanzibar retains a strong Muslim character: women wear burqas or veils, while men are dressed in kofia and kanzu.

However, what also strikes me, as in many Eastern countries I've had the chance to visit, is the neglect of waste management. Piles of garbage accumulate everywhere, and no one seems to care… except the chickens pecking through the debris. In Stone Town, the old town listed as a UNESCO World Heritage Site, we were guided through a maze of alleys, discovering a truly different world.

After twelve days in national parks, it was time to relax: pool, sea, and leisure... No more red, yellow, or grey dust clinging to our skin and filling every corner of our bodies. What luxury to enjoy a fan instead of those tent flaps through which the violent winds of the dry season crash in, making the canvas flap and the wooden structure creak. We chose four nights under canvas in the parks and the rest of the time in lodges located in the heart of the reserves, where guards would escort us. Some were armed with bows and arrows, others with old rifles—each adding to the atmosphere.

The atmosphere was straight out of a movie, almost as if we were actors in Out of Africa. The lodges were a mix of colonial and African styles, built and decorated with local materials. Each night, we had the choice of a cabin, a cottage, or even a tent, sometimes with two double beds and a full bathroom. And, of course, the views were breathtaking.

Imagine a giraffe slowly grazing right in front of your balcony, or a lion roaring just meters from your tent wall. The nights were both thrilling and exhausting.

I came here with one goal: to see the "Big Five"—elephants, rhinos, leopards, lions, and buffalo, once prized by hunters as trophies. But what I really discovered was a true life lesson. Africa bewitched me, and to me, Tanzania embodies the real Africa: endless steppes, golden bushland dotted with ancient baobabs and acacias—

the umbrella trees where animals find refuge from the searing sun.

The images of the wildlife will stay with me forever: elephants walking in single file with their calves nestled beneath them, thousands of gazelles fleeing in all directions, monkeys squabbling, a hyena devouring a carcass under the watchful eyes of hungry vultures, a leopard perched on a branch, lionesses with cubs rubbing against them, majestic giraffes strutting, buffalo glaring at us with threatening eyes, wildebeest and zebras running as far as the eye could see, a rare solitary rhino, hundreds of hippos bellowing in the water...

But there are also the Maasai. You meet them everywhere, their red and purple robes dotting the landscape as they walk with herds of goats, cows, or cattle in search of pasture. It's common to see young boys, barely ten or twelve years old, herding fifty animals. We saw hundreds, with their herds and small villages. The Maasai are still very present in the region, but they dislike being photographed. They are not a spectacle for us, foreigners in their realm.

Tucked in the middle of Southern Africa, the Caprivi Strip is a unique stopover, a strange and fascinating territory where you pass through countless bush villages. This journey offered a rare opportunity to discover another side of the region— an authentic Africa, off the beaten path, where traditions have endured for centuries.

The highlight of this adventure was visiting the iconic site where the famous film The Gods Must Be Crazy was shot. This cult classic tells the story of a tribe in the Kalahari Desert, isolated from the modern world, whose lives are upended when a Coca-Cola bottle falls from the sky. A simple object for us becomes a symbol of discord and questioning—a metaphor for the clash between two opposing worlds.

To reach this legendary place, we undertook a grueling journey: eight hours on bumpy tracks through arid and majestic landscapes. Once there, we spent the night in a basic tent, without modern comforts—no shower, no amenities. Far from a simple inconvenience, this immersion deepened our experience of the place, making it all the more authentic.

At dawn, exactly at six o'clock, we were up and ready for an expedition into the bush. One hour of travel by jeep and on foot brought us to the Bushmen's village—these hunter-gatherers who have lived in harmony with nature for millennia.

From the moment we arrived, they welcomed us with curiosity and kindness. In a burst of friendliness, they adorned me with a traditional wig—a custom likely meant to integrate us temporarily into their way of life. Then we went hunting, equipped with rudimentary bows and arrows, accompanied by several dogs trained to track game. Observing their ability to read tracks, lay ambushes, and adapt to their environment was fascinating.

Every gesture seemed ancient, passed down from generation to generation, untouched by modernity.

After this intense expedition, we shared a moment of relaxation with them. They smoked a local herb, similar to marijuana, and offered it to me. I politely declined, preferring instead to gift them a few cigars. Their faces lit up with gratitude, and they accepted them with enthusiasm, enjoying them as a treasured surprise.

This journey was far more than just exploration—it was a dive into an age-old culture, an adventure where every moment was a lesson in life. Far from the turmoil of the modern world, in the heart of the Kalahari Desert, we touched a forgotten truth: a simple existence in harmony with nature, where every object, every gesture, every rite carries deep meaning.

Victoria Falls: A Cinematic Dream Come True

Everyone from my generation remembers Tarzan, Johnny Weissmuller, and the legendary scene where he dives into Victoria Falls. Back then, it was fiction—a distant and exotic backdrop that made us dream from our movie seats. But today, that dream has become my reality.

I dreamed of discovering that legendary place. And one day, I went.

When I finally set foot at Victoria Falls, on the border between Zambia and Zimbabwe, a shiver ran through me. The vastness, the roar of the water, the mist rising to the sky... it all defied imagination. Nothing can truly prepare you for the raw power of that one-kilometer-wide wall of water where the Zambezi River plunges with incredible force.

I stood there, soaked in the eternal spray, wide-eyed and moved. This was no longer a cinema. This was my life.

Our guide shared a fascinating story: during the dry season, elephants sometimes cross the riverbed on foot in search of water. Yes, elephants walking through the nearly dried-out bed of Victoria Falls! That image struck me—these peaceful giants slowly advancing through a place as sacred as it is spectacular, as if they were its true guardians.

These majestic falls, located at the border of Zimbabwe and Zambia, left me speechless. With a width of more than 1,700 meters and a height of 108 meters, they are twice the size of Niagara Falls. Their deafening roar can be heard from miles away. The mist that rises, visible from nearly 20 kilometers, is one of the most impressive sights I have ever seen.

The falls, nicknamed Mosi-oa-Tunya or "The Smoke That Thunders," are a true natural monument, surrounded by wild fauna. Elephants, hippos, crocodiles... nature reigns supreme in this timeless place. After marveling at the power of the falls, we continued our adventure through the safaris of Botswana and Zimbabwe, encountering the Big Five: lions, leopards, elephants, buffalo, and rhinos. Each safari was an immersion into a raw and fascinating world.

Chapter 36: The Adventure

Céline Dion performed in Singapore during her Céline Dion Live 2018 Tour on July 3 and 4, 2018, at the prestigious Marina Bay Sands Grand Hotel. I had seen the news report, and at that moment, a dream was born within me.

At 75 years old, I set foot on these paradise islands. On December 30, 2020, we flew from Miami to Singapore—a journey that would mark the beginning of an extraordinary adventure.

Singapore: A Futuristic and Refined Jewel

We spent four days at the Marina Bay Sands Hotel, a place as monumental as it is fascinating. Shaped like a ship resting atop three glass towers, it towers over the city. Its infinity pool, suspended on the 57th floor, is probably one of the most photographed in the world. Swimming in this iconic pool, 200 meters above ground, with the Singapore skyline as a backdrop, was a surreal experience. The feeling of floating between sky and sea, surrounded by illuminated skyscrapers, made us feel as if we were dreaming with our eyes open.

Singapore is a world apart—an ultra-modern, clean, and astonishingly well-organized city-state where Asian tradition coexists harmoniously with technological innovation. During the day, we explored its multicultural neighborhoods: Chinatown with its colorful temples, Little India and its fragrant markets, and Kampong Glam and its elegant mosques. Each district was an immersion into a different universe, and everywhere, Singaporean refinement captivated us.

We also visited Gardens by the Bay, a futuristic park with "giant trees" covered in tropical plants. At nightfall, a sound and light show transformed these structures into living sculptures. The contrast between nature, modernity, and architectural design is everywhere in Singapore—and that's what makes it so unique.

But what we were most looking forward to was the famous evening of December 31. We had booked a table on the SkyPark of the hotel, the panoramic rooftop overlooking the bay. Everything was exceptional: a gourmet buffet, an elegant and electric ambiance, and above all, a breathtaking visual show. Laser beams streaked the sky, light projections danced on the buildings' façades, and fireworks lit up the Marina in rhythm with the music. It wasn't just a celebration—it was a celestial choreography.

That night, in that space suspended between sky and sea, we said goodbye to a strange year and welcomed the new one with wonder and gratitude.

Marina Bay Sands Hotel

Indian Ocean and Vietnam Cruise

After the dazzling lights of Singapore and the unforgettable New Year's celebration atop Marina Bay Sands, our adventure continued to wilder, more secret shores. On January 4, we boarded a cruise ship, heading to four islands with distinct personalities: Madagascar, Seychelles, Mauritius, and Réunion. Four pearls set on the Indian Ocean, each offering a unique immersion into nature, culture, and humanity.

Madagascar – The Island of a Thousand Faces

First stop: Madagascar—vast, mysterious, and deeply authentic. The contrast was striking: here, everything remains raw, vibrant, and untamed. Nature reigns supreme. Our journey began in Antananarivo, a capital perched on steep hills. Then we left the city for more remote areas where time seems to stand still. What marks you here isn't the hotels or infrastructure—it's the children's smiles, the spontaneous kindness, the sincere gazes. On Morondava's red tracks, we drove to the Avenue of the Baobabs. At sunset, the silhouettes of these ancient giants against the amber sky were unforgettable.

Seychelles – Between Sky, Sea, and Granite

"Emmanuelle" and her husband, lost in their torrid passions under the sensual sun of Seychelles, left an indelible impression on me. I was 32 when I first saw the film. The aesthetic of the setting, the softness of the white sand, the endless turquoise sea, and the sensual freedom of the place left a deep mark. It wasn't just cinema—it was a call to travel, to awaken the senses, to fulfill an exotic dream. That day, I made myself a promise: one day, I too would live in the Seychelles.

That dream lay dormant for a long time, lulled by years of work, projects, and responsibilities. But it remained intact, like a spark waiting. At 75, while many close the door on dreams, I opened it wide. And I set course for this Indian Ocean paradise, eyes filled with hope, heart beating like a young man.

A Day in a Living Postcard

The dream came to life on La Digue, the jewel of the Seychelles. We spent only one day there, but what a day! From the moment we arrived, I felt like I had stepped into a living postcard. Anse Source d'Argent beach, which I had seen countless times in photos, lay before me in its unreal splendor. Giant granite boulders polished by time, resting like sculptures on powdery sand, bathed by an incredibly clear turquoise sea.

I sat for a moment, simply to breathe, observe, and absorb. I was no longer a traveler; I was a fulfilled witness. Everything I had imagined watching Emmanuelle on that distant screen was here—real, tangible. It wasn't a dream coming true—it was a dream embracing me.

We walked barefoot, swam, and laughed. I looked back several times to imprint those images in my memory. I knew I would stay just one day, but I had decided that this day would last forever in my mind.

Mauritius – A Harmonious Blend of Cultures

Mauritius welcomed us with warmth, smiles, and elegance. A true crossroads of cultures—Indian, Creole, European, and Chinese—coexisting with admirable harmony. We drove across the island, from the lively market of Port Louis to the multicolored lands of Chamarel, and the tea plantations of Bois Chéri. In the evening, by the lagoon, we enjoyed spiced curries or chilli cakes while listening to musicians play Sega.

Réunion – Land of Fire and Awe

Our final Indian Ocean stop was Réunion, a French island both wild and spectacular. The mountainous cirques of Cilaos and Mafate, cascading waterfalls, lush forests, and the Piton de la Fournaise all evoked dramatic natural beauty. We met passionate, generous, and proud Réunionnais people.

Vietnam: Memory, Courage, and Natural Splendor

In Vietnam, the adventure took on a deeper tone, rich with emotion, sharp contrasts, and moving discoveries.

In Hanoi, I rode a cycle through bustling alleys, immersed in the vibrant chaos of the city. Horns honking, incense and street food smells, markets bursting with energy—everything pulsed with an electric intensity. Every street corner told a story.

Next, we headed south to Ho Chi Minh City for a visit to the War Remnants Museum. There, the shock was visceral. The images, objects, and testimonies... all evoked the raw horror of conflict. This museum is no mere exhibit—it confronts you with the cruelest forms of human suffering. You leave shaken, heart heavy with injustice and sorrow. How could a people survive such devastation and still smile with dignity today? Vietnam teaches resilience at every step.

But the story didn't end there. We then visited the Cu Chi tunnels, a network of ingenious and oppressive underground passages used by Vietnamese fighters during the war. To understand their daily life, you had to experience it. I wanted to go down myself. Very quickly, I found myself stuck in a narrow tunnel. Air was scarce, darkness suffocating. My heart pounded wildly. Crawling on all fours, in silence, through that tight earthen gallery... a claustrophobic, intense, yet enlightening experience.

Finally, to end our Vietnamese immersion, we set sail on a traditional wooden boat to the famous Ha Long Bay. Between its spectacular karst formations rising from the waters like sleeping dragons and its mystical mists floating above the surface, the place felt unreal. But it was by leaving the tourist paths that the magic fully unfolded: we sailed to the secluded Bai Tu Long Bay—peaceful, silent, almost beyond time. A final breath of pure beauty to conclude a deeply human journey.

From Singapore to Madagascar, from Seychelles to Réunion, and from Mauritius to Vietnam, this cruise was more than just a trip: it was a journey through the world's contrasts and wonders. Each stop transformed us a little, reminding us how vast, beautiful, and precious our planet is. We didn't just travel with suitcases, but with wide-open hearts.

PART FOUR

Chapter 37: Adventure Travel

India: 25 Days for a Second Discovery

I had already written about my first trip to India, but this time, I had the opportunity to visit Mumbai. Among the most striking discoveries was Dhobi Ghat, the world's largest open-air laundry.

A true human anthill, where hundreds of dhobis—the washers—work tirelessly from morning to evening. Shirts, sheets, uniforms— everything goes through their hands. Clothes are scrubbed by hand, beaten on stones, rinsed in large vats, and then hung on endless ropes stretched under the sun. It's hard to believe that in such a modern metropolis, this traditional ritual still endures, unchanged for over a century.

But it was on returning to my hotel that the contrast struck me head-on.

I had chosen to stay at the Taj Mahal Palace, a legendary establishment located opposite the Gateway of India. With its colonial architecture, elegant dome, and rich history, the hotel embodies a blend of luxury and cultural heritage. Walking through its marble hallways, I felt transported back to the days of the British Raj.

Mumbai is a city of contrasts. Ultra-modern skyscrapers coexist with slums. Limousines cross paths with rickshaws. The noise, the colors, the smells—it's a sensory shock. Yet it's also a place where spirituality and technology meet. Temples nestled between towers. Monks with smartphones.

I also explored the Elephanta Caves, located on an island in Mumbai's harbor. The boat ride was short but pleasant. The caves house magnificent rock sculptures, dedicated mainly to the god Shiva. The serenity of the site, combined with the craftsmanship of the carvings, left a deep impression on me.

A memorable moment was discovering the tower of Mukesh Ambani, the richest man in India (€115 billion) and in Asia.

His vast private residence, known as Antilia, has 27 floors and spans 400,000 square feet. This architectural masterpiece is worth over $2 billion and includes four floors of garages for his numerous cars.

India is a land of contrasts, where wealth and poverty live side by side. In Kolkata, we visited Mother Teresa's headquarters, then the Gandhi Museum in New Delhi.

A Breakfast at the Top of the World

The end of our journey in Nepal was marked by an extraordinary experience: a helicopter flight into the heart of the Himalayas, to the outskirts of the mythical Everest Base Camp.

We took off from Kathmandu at dawn, as the city slowly awakened under a veil of mist. After a technical stop in Lukla—a tiny airport clinging to the mountainside—to lighten the aircraft, we resumed our ascent toward the snowy peaks.

As we gained altitude, the air grew thinner, and the pilot calmly put on his oxygen mask. He turned to us with a half-smile and said a phrase I will never forget:

"At this altitude, the most important thing is the pilot."

We understood there was no room for error.

The spectacle was surreal. Before our eyes, the highest mountains in the world unfolded like a frozen ocean. The trails were visible from afar, dotted with tiny figures: brave hikers taking step after step toward their Everest dream.

Then, around a ridge, the Everest View Hotel appeared, reputed to be the highest hotel in the world accessible by helicopter. There, at 3,880 meters altitude, we enjoyed a hot breakfast facing the world's most famous peaks: Ama Dablam, Lhotse, Nuptse, and, of course, Everest itself. It was more than a meal; it was a moment suspended in eternity. The silence, the pure light, the sensation of being so close to the sky... A dream come true, forever etched in my memory.

This contrast between the luxury of the Taj and the harsh daily life of the washermen embodies, in itself, the very essence of India: a land of extremes, of inequalities, but also of beauty, pride, and resilience.

Three Paradises, Three Worlds

Traveling means discovering unknown worlds, letting oneself be surprised by the raw beauty of nature, and immersing oneself in distant cultures. Among all the places I've explored, three islands lost in the heart of the oceans have offered me unforgettable experiences: the Maldives, Tahiti, and the Galápagos Islands.

The Maldives: The Azure Dream

Located in the Indian Ocean, southwest of Sri Lanka and India, the Maldives form an archipelago of 1,200 coral islands grouped into 26 natural atolls. These paradise islands, of which only about 200 are inhabited, stretch like a necklace of pearls over unreal blue waters. From the air, the perfect geometry of the atolls looks like a natural work of art.

From the moment I arrived, I was struck by the surreal clarity of the waters, the intensity of the lagoon's blue, and the soft warmth of the sea air. Time seemed to stand still, as if every second was worth an hour of contemplation. Each morning, I would dive from my terrace to explore the coral reefs. Tropical fish, manta rays, and even reef sharks swam fearlessly in these protected waters. It felt like swimming in a living aquarium.

What sets the Maldives apart from other tropical paradises is its absolute peace. The archipelago invites luxurious seclusion, far from the chaos of the world. The silence is complete, broken only by the rustling of palm trees and the lapping of water against the stilts. I found a rare serenity there, almost meditative. The noise of the world had vanished.

Every late afternoon offered a celestial spectacle. The sunsets turned the sky into a gradient of gold and pink, then gave way to a starry night of absolute purity. No streetlights, no pollution—just the Milky Way, clear and majestic.

Why Go?

- To sleep above the sea in a stilt bungalow—a signature luxury of the Maldives.

  - To dive or snorkel in one of the world's most stunning coral ecosystems.
  - To recharge in total calm, far from crowds and noise.
  - To enjoy a full sensory experience: sight, sound, touch, and smell—all heightened.
  - To observe rare marine species like hawksbill turtles, dolphins, or giant rays.

The Maldives are about 700 km southwest of Sri Lanka in the Indian Ocean. Most travelers arrive via Malé International Airport, then transfer to island resorts by seaplane or speedboat.

The Promise of Another World

French Polynesia carried me into a waking dream. This journey was not simply something I experienced—it was something I felt, in my skin, in my breath, and in my soul.

Tahiti welcomed me with the scent of tiare flowers and its warm, inviting atmosphere. But my Polynesian voyage took on an even more magical dimension when I embarked on a seven-day cruise aboard the Paul Gauguin, an intimate ship designed to navigate the heart of paradise.

During this voyage, I discovered the jewels of Polynesia: Moorea, with its majestic mountains plunging into a lagoon painted in a thousand shades of blue; Bora Bora, the legendary island where I swam with stingrays and blacktip reef sharks in crystalline waters; Huahine, wild and mysterious, where time seems to stand still.

Days aboard the ship flowed gently to the rhythm of the sea, between stops at paradisiacal isles, lectures on Polynesian culture, and evenings enchanted by the music of ukuleles. Each sunrise delivered its own marvels, and each sunset painted the sky with an entrancing palette.

Why Go to Polynesia?

Because Tahiti and its neighboring islands are much more than postcards, they form a world where land, sea, and sky exist in harmony, each element speaking a forgotten language—the language of silence, pure beauty, and rediscovered slow living.

It's a place to reconnect with oneself but also to listen to ancient tales—legends passed down beneath the stars by Polynesian navigators who traversed the ocean guided by stars, wind, and currents.

Tahiti: The Beating Heart

In Tahiti, everything begins at the vibrant markets of Papeete, with stalls overflowing with flowers, tropical fruits, and the intoxicating smell of vanilla. But the true treasure lies in the landscapes:

steep, jungle-clad mountains, hidden waterfalls, and black sand beaches washed by the Pacific Ocean.

The lagoon on the west coast offers an early taste of enchantment, and inland, the lush valleys tell another tale—of the preserved interior of a volcanic island, raw and generous in its natural beauty.

Moorea: The Sister Island

Moorea is so close to Tahiti that you can reach it by ferry in less than an hour—but it feels like another world. Its razor-edged peaks plunge dramatically into the sea, creating fairytale scenery. The lagoon is a living aquarium, where you can swim with rays and reef sharks, or simply marvel at the kaleidoscope of corals while snorkeling.

On land, you'll find pineapple plantations, traditional villages, and breathtaking viewpoints like the Moorea lookout, where the twin bays of Opunohu and Cook unfold beneath you.

Bora Bora: The Pearl of the Pacific

Bora Bora is the myth made reality. A central island surrounded by a turquoise lagoon encircled itself with a coral barrier. This unreal landscape is dotted with motus—small sandy islets, often untouched, sometimes hosting luxury overwater bungalows.

Yet beyond the luxury lies breathtaking nature. I swam with stingrays, watched blacktip reef sharks glide beneath my mask, and walked on beaches so pristine they felt untouched by any footstep.

The island's interior, dominated by Mount Otemanu, is reachable by hiking or 4×4, revealing dense vegetation, historical remains, and spectacular views over the lagoon.

Huahine: The Secret Island

Huahine surprised me. Less frequented than Bora Bora or Moorea, it granted me the intimacy of the true traveler. Here, you discover quiet villages, fishermen still carving their own outrigger canoes, and Polynesian archaeological sites (marae) that bear witness to an ancient culture.

It's an island that embodies the human–nature connection, where time seems to flow more slowly.

The Galápagos Islands: Sanctuary of Time

When I chose to visit Ecuador, that small country nestled along the equator, I had no idea it would become such a revelation for me. Ecuador is one of South America's best-kept secrets—a stable, welcoming nation where the high quality of life and low cost of living have made it a favorite among retirees from Europe and North America. With its charming colonial cities like Cuenca and Quito, majestic mountains, Amazon rainforest, and peaceful beaches, Ecuador has much to offer curious minds. But it was the Galápagos Islands that truly drew me across the Pacific Ocean.

Located nearly 1,000 kilometers off Ecuador's coast, this legendary archipelago is one of the last places on Earth where nature still reigns supreme. A UNESCO World Heritage Site, the Galápagos are far more than a travel destination—they are a living laboratory of evolution. It's no coincidence that Charles Darwin developed his theory of natural selection here.

If Tahiti stirred my soul and the Maldives brought me serenity, the Galápagos awed me in an entirely different way—by reconnecting me to nature in its rawest, purest, most untamed form.

Here, there is no luxury, no artifice. Everything is real. Everything is alive.

To walk alongside hundred-year-old giant tortoises, to see marine iguanas dive into the waves as if challenging the ocean, to witness blue-footed boobies perform their courtship dances with innocence and grace—it felt like stepping into a world before mankind. Nowhere else have I witnessed such a coexistence between humans and wildlife, in a balance as delicate as it is precious.

On these islands, I felt a deep sense of humility. In the presence of such magnificent life—creatures that have never learned to fear humans, I became aware of a fundamental truth: our planet is not something to be conquered, but something to be respected. Every rock, every animal, every breath of wind reminded me that nature does not belong to us—we are simply a part of it, and only for a brief moment.

How to Get There

From mainland Ecuador, two daily flights connect Quito or Guayaquil to the archipelago, typically landing in Baltra or San Cristóbal. It's advisable to spend a few days on the mainland to acclimate before flying to the Galápagos.

Cruise or Land Stay?

I chose an expedition cruise: a small vessel with a dozen cabins that allowed us to access several islands in peace and quiet. Each day, a naturalist guide took us to encounter unique wildlife—sea lions, penguins, white-tip reef sharks, red-footed boobies, flightless cormorants...

Those who prefer to stay on land can find lodging in the villages of Puerto Ayora or Puerto Baquerizo Moreno, with day trips available to nearby islands.

Best Time to Visit?

There's no bad season. From January to May, the sea is calm and the landscapes are lush and green. From June to December, the water is cooler, but marine life is even more active. I visited in March: the temperatures were perfect, the skies clear, and the animals... everywhere.

What I Brought Back from This Journey

I returned without material souvenirs but with a transformed perspective. Seeing nature so confident, so unwary of human presence, moved me deeply. It was one of the few times in my life where I truly felt like a guest—not a master—of the place.

The Galápagos are not a destination to be consumed. They are islands for learning, for wonder, and above all… for silence and listening.

Three Journeys, Three Lessons

Each of these places gave me a lesson. The Maldives taught me the luxury of silence, Tahiti the richness of tradition, and the Galápagos the importance of harmony with nature. Three islands, three experiences, three ways of existing in this world.

And through these journeys, I have learned to listen, to observe, and to appreciate beauty in all its forms.

At 78, Still in the American West

Arriving in Calgary by plane, we spent the first night at the Hilton Garden Inn, eagerly awaiting the delivery of my bike. The next day, the adventure started: heading toward Banff, the jewel of the Canadian Rockies, where Lake Louise offers its unforgettable spectacle—turquoise waters framed by snow-capped peaks.

From Hot Springs to the Vast Expanses of Montana

Our first extended stop was at Radium Hot Springs, on the legendary Route 93. Two days soaking in the thermal waters, perfect for releasing tension before the grand descent into the United States.

After passing through customs, we plunged straight into the majestic world of Glacier National Park in Montana. The winding roads of the Going-to-the-Sun Road reveal vertigo-inducing panoramas, where glaciers, deep valleys, and waterfalls follow one another in an almost unreal setting.

Wyoming and the Wonders of Yellowstone

The journey continued into Wyoming, land of Yellowstone, the United States' first national park. Along the way, we stopped at Cody, a town founded by none other than Buffalo Bill. Its Western ambiance and rodeo museum immerse you in the history of the Old West.

Yellowstone is an explosion of wild nature: the Old Faithful geyser, Mammoth Hot Springs, Grand Prismatic Spring, and, of course, the impressive bison herds roaming the plains. The experience is unforgettable. Leaving the park, we stopped in Jackson, a town where the cowboy spirit remains alive and well.

Colorado, Texas, and the Legendary Route 66

A change of scenery with Rocky Mountain National Park, where roads rise amid snowy peaks and green valleys. Then we headed to Texas, passing through Amarillo and its famous Cadillac

Ranch, where car carcasses embedded in the ground serve as canvases for travelers' graffiti.

Utah, Motorcyclist's Paradise

Utah is a dream for motorcycle enthusiasts. Mexican Hat, a village lost between desert and cliffs, announces the arrival at Four Corners, the unique point where Utah, Arizona, New Mexico, and Colorado meet. But the most spectacular place remains Moab and its Arches National Park, where giant stone arches sculpted by time offer an almost lunar landscape.

As we continued, we crossed the legendary Bryce Canyon, Zion National Park, and then arrived at one of the most iconic sites in the West: Monument Valley. This Western film backdrop, with its colossal monoliths…

Monument Valley

It's impossible to pass through Arizona without stopping at the Grand Canyon, that dizzying chasm carved by the Colorado River. Further on, we discovered the mysterious Meteor Crater, evidence of a meteor impact over 50,000 years ago. The road then led us to Sedona, where red rocks contrast with the brilliant blue sky.

After so many kilometers across mountains and deserts, a well-deserved three-day rest at Desert Hot

Springs in California offered relaxation and serenity.

Before the final stretch, we made a detour to the colossal Hoover Dam, an engineering masterpiece holding back the waters of Lake Mead. Then came the arrival in Las Vegas, the city of lights and contrasts, where we savored the end of this adventure.

After 8,570 km of a memorable ride, my faithful motorcycle was shipped back to Quebec, while we returned with our heads full of images and lasting memories.

This journey at 78 was not just a ride, but a statement that the spirit of adventure knows no age.

Newfoundland, 79 Years Old

I wanted to mark the occasion with a final grand motorcycle journey. With my faithful automatic Goldwing, we left Montreal on June 30, 2024, heading to Rimouski. There, we boarded the

Nordic, a ship bound for Blanc Sablon over five days, with my bike safely stowed in a container.

The sea voyage was an adventure in itself. Each stop revealed new landscapes and a new atmosphere. In Sept Îles, feeling the raw presence of the river—this vastness reminded me how expansive and majestic Quebec is. Anticosti Island, wild and mysterious, offered the fascinating sight of deer living freely. At Havre Saint Pierre, we admired the monoliths of Mingan Archipelago National Park, sculpted by time and erosion.

Then came Kegaska, a small, remote outpost where one feels the weight of isolation and the strength of its inhabitants. At Harrington Harbor, we discovered a time-frozen village, with wooden streets and no cars—the impression of another century. I found myself imagining life here, paced by the sea and the seasons. It was a striking stop, made even more poignant by its link to the film La Grande Séduction, which was shot here.

The other stops—Tête à la Baleine, La Tabatière, and Saint Augustin—allowed conversations with exceptionally generous people living at a rhythm lost to big cities. Then, finally, Blanc Sablon. There, my motorcycle was unloaded, and we crossed to Labrador.

Arriving in Sainte Barbe, we set our wheels on Newfoundland soil. The bracing, salty air gave us energy to continue the adventure. We headed to L'Anse aux Meadows, a fascinating historic site where Vikings established a settlement over a thousand years ago. Then to St. Anthony, to see icebergs drifting slowly offshore—silent witnesses to a changing world.

Gros Morne National Park was another highlight of the journey. Its raw beauty—mountains and fjords—shows how nature can be both peaceful and imposing. Every turn on its winding roads was like a new postcard; every stop, a moment of wonder.

After crossing Newfoundland, we took the ferry from Port aux Basques to North Sydney, Nova Scotia. From there, we traveled to Charlottetown, Prince Edward Island, with its rolling landscapes and pastel colored homes. Then, through New Brunswick, before returning to Quebec, completing a journey of over 3,000 kilometers.

But this journey was also a revelation. I understood that, despite my undiminished passion for motorcycles, such adventures now demand too much energy. Planning routes, managing long distances, finding hotels and restaurants, and facing the unexpected… it had become exhausting.

So yes, I will continue to ride, but differently. From now on, they will be shorter getaways—one or two days—just for the pleasure of feeling the wind, the road, the freedom.

Aging is accepting slowing down. It's mourning certain things while remaining true to oneself. This journey will remain etched in me as the last of an era… and the beginning of a new one.

3886 feet

Mount Washington: A Final Challenge

In September 2024, at 79, I finally achieved a dream: riding up Mount Washington on my motorcycle. I had often been warned about the danger of the road, but the experience was worth every moment. Climbing through the trees, then reaching the summit to admire a spectacular panorama… a true moment of pride.

This chapter retraces unforgettable moments but also marks a transition in my way of traveling. Today, I favor shorter adventures, but no less intense.

Chapter 38: Aging

Throughout my life, I have heard this phrase hundreds of times: "I should have…" Too late. The train has passed, and it will not return. One never regrets what one dared. One regrets what one did not try.

I always believed that by giving a lot, one inevitably did good. But one day, a simple plant gave me an unexpected lesson. It died. Not from neglect, but because I had given it too much water. Too much love, sometimes, can suffocate instead of nourish. I then understood that giving too much can prevent growth.

At 79, I made a significant donation to the Garde-Manger des Pays-d'en-Haut. Not for applause. No. To answer a visceral need I felt: simply to help those who are hungry.

At 80, one question arises: And now?

Today, I think more about myself. We must be realistic: how many years do I have left?

Why have I not spoken here about my family or personal life? This silence is intentional. This book is not an intimate confession. It is the journey of a man who sought to understand, to build, to transmit. My dreams and desires have been expressed through commitment, through ideas, through action.

I loved my family in my own way. I gave everything I could, sometimes too much like that plant, drowned by excess attention. But I regret nothing. What was given was given with tenderness and generosity. I hope I have passed on some of my passions to my two sons and five grandchildren. I traveled with them many times. Each of my grandchildren even had a trip with me.

Unlike many politicians, I lived with a passion for politics from a very young age, and it deeply shaped my life.

I have lived a full life—sometimes harsh, often intense—always guided by this inner force: the desire to move forward, to dream, to live according to what I believed was right. If this book can inspire, question, or simply touch, then it will have fulfilled its mission.

But now, at nearly 80, I realize that aging also means learning to let go.

I lost my parents. We were three children, and I am the youngest. One of my sisters has already gone. Traveling as before has become difficult. Gone are the motorcycle adventures, gone are the grand projects that require energy I no longer have. One becomes more cautious and avoids financial risks. Aging is knowing how to adapt, how to accept change. Fortunately, life gave me the courage to accomplish everything while I still had the strength.

The writer Marc Lévy wrote: "One can blame one's childhood." One can endlessly accuse one's parents of all the woes that burden us. But ultimately, we are responsible for our own existence. "We become what we have decided to be."

I decided to live according to the great lessons of life that allowed me to achieve my dreams and desires. And I firmly believe that the more one accomplishes, the less one thinks about age. Aging also means better understanding one's past, freeing oneself from old wounds, and moving forward with wisdom.

This book is the testimony of all that is behind me. But what will my future be? As always, I let life surprise me. Aging is not a hindrance, but an opportunity to evolve, again and again. Throughout my life, I learned to turn challenges into lessons, to savor each moment, and to nurture my dreams so I could transform them into reality. Today, at 80, I realize that the important thing is not how much time we have left, but how we choose to live it.

Writing has become my new adventure, a journey without limits or borders. I still feel this passion, this inner fire that has always guided me, and I know I still have so many stories to tell. This book is not a conclusion, but a springboard toward a new horizon. It marks the end of one chapter, but certainly not the end of the book of my life.

Aging also means transmitting. Leaving behind a legacy—not only material, but above all immaterial: values, experiences, memories, lessons. I am proud of what I have accomplished, but even more of what I have shared. My greatest wish is that these pages inspire those who will read them, that they remind everyone that life is an endless sequence of possibilities, as long as one dares to dream and act.

Aging is a privilege. A journey I continue with gratitude, with the certainty that the best is always yet to come.

Night falls slowly, wrapping the landscape in gentle darkness. Sitting on my rocking chair, a steaming cup of honey in my hands, I let my mind wander down the paths of the past. Every evening, this ritual offered me a pause, a moment of respite from the day's turmoil.

I had spent the day sorting through old memories, letters yellowed by time, photographs worn at the edges—relics of a time when every instant seemed to hold infinite promise. Among these relics, one letter caught my attention. Its ink was faded, but the words still resonated with poignant intensity: "Never stop dreaming, for it is in your dreams that the essence of your freedom resides." These words, written by someone who had marked my life, stirred a flood of emotions within me. They reminded me how much dreams had always guided my steps, pushing me to dare, to believe in the impossible. There had been failures, disappointments, but also countless victories, small and great.

I lifted my eyes to the sky, sprinkled with shining stars. Each seemed to carry a fragment of my hopes, of my aspirations. The past was a compass, but the future was my destination. There was still so much to accomplish, so much to explore.

Breathing deeply the fresh night air, I smiled. The road ahead was still long, but I knew it was worth traveling. For as long as there are dreams, there is a reason to move forward.

So, what to do at 80? For some time now, an idea has been growing within me: to write a novel.

And if that were my next great project?

I gently close this book, but I do not close the door to my dreams. They remain—always. As long as the heart beats, as long as the eyes shine, there is a road to travel.

And you? What are your hidden dreams? Perhaps a journey never taken, a project postponed, a passion forgotten?

Do not wait for tomorrow. Begin today. The most beautiful gift we can give ourselves is to live our dreams before they become regrets.

Acknowledgments

I offer my heartfelt thanks to my family, the foundation of my strength and dreams.

I am grateful for the life that challenged and blessed me in equal measure.

To all who crossed my path—who believed, encouraged, or guided me—this book carries a part of you.

About The Author

Ronald Bussey never waited—he made things happen. As alderman, executive vice-president of Laval, and founder of the PRO party that defeated the incumbent mayor, he proved that daring can change the course of events.

A bold entrepreneur, he built landmark projects: the Faubourg, the Factoreries Saint-Sauveur, developments on the land of Séraphin Saint-Adèle, and mini-warehouses north of Mirabel. He also offered second chances through private loans.

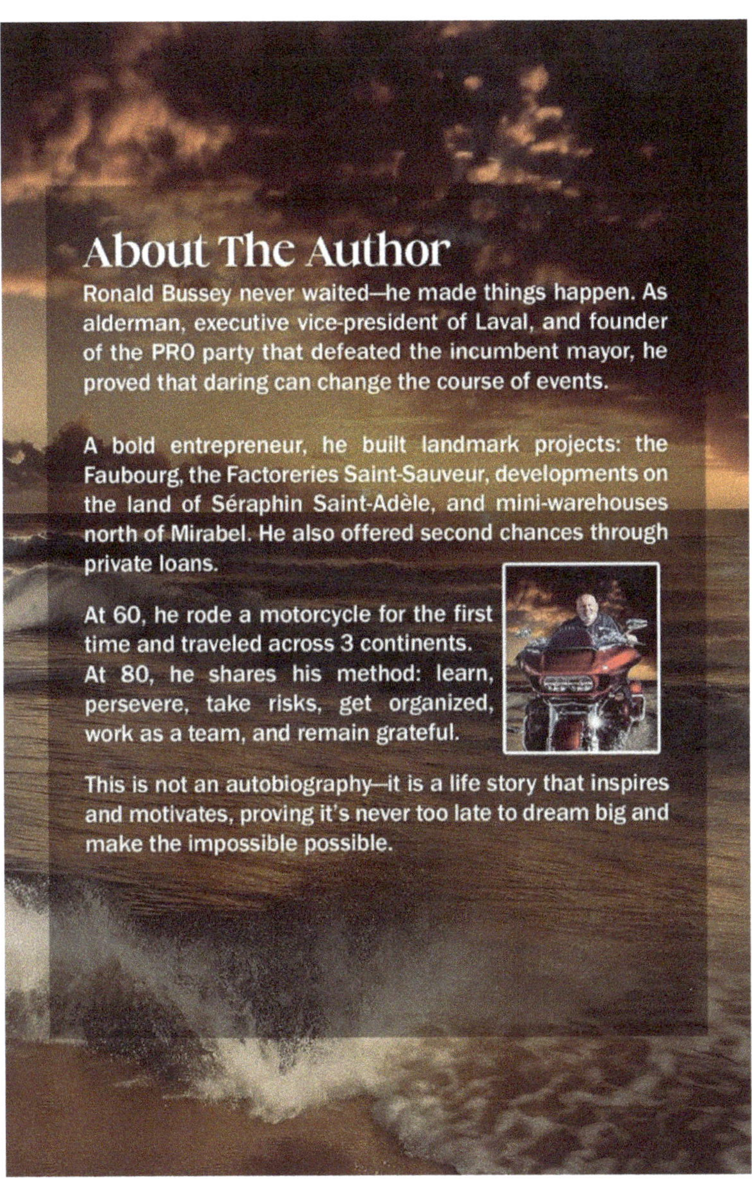

At 60, he rode a motorcycle for the first time and traveled across 3 continents.
At 80, he shares his method: learn, persevere, take risks, get organized, work as a team, and remain grateful.

This is not an autobiography—it is a life story that inspires and motivates, proving it's never too late to dream big and make the impossible possible.